THE PRAISE
OF
FOLLY

THE PRAISE
OF
FOLLY

DESIDERIUS
ERASMUS
Translated by John Wilson

GREAT MINDS SERIES

Prometheus Books

59 John Glenn Drive
Amherst, New York 14228-2197

Published 1994 by Prometheus Books
59 John Glenn Drive, Amherst, New York 14228-2197.
716-691-0133. FAX: 716-691-0137.

Library of Congress Cataloging-in-Publication Data

Erasmus, Desiderius, d. 1536.
    [Moriae encomium. English]
    The praise of folly / Desiderius Erasmus ; translated by John Wilson.
        p.   cm. — (Great minds series)
    Originally published: Oxford : Clarendon Press, 1913.
    ISBN 0-87975-885-6 (pbk.)
    1. Folly—Religious aspects—Christianity. I. Wilson, John, 1627?–1696.
II. Title. III. Series.
PA8514.E5   1994
873′.04—dc20   94-5475
                                                               CIP

Printed in Canada on acid-free paper.

Also Available in Prometheus's Great Minds Paperback Series

See the back of this volume for a complete list of titles in Prometheus's Great Books in Philosophy and Great Minds series.

DESIDERIUS ERASMUS was born at Rotterdam, of an unwed mother, on October 27, 1466. Erasmus' father provided for his son's early education, sending him first to the cathedral school of Utrecht and afterward to the famous school of Deventer. Following the premature deaths of both parents, Erasmus was placed by his guardians at the preparatory school in Hertogenbosch; thereafter he entered the novitiate in a house of the regular canon of St. Augustine at Stein near Gouda. Erasmus was solemnly professed, at age nineteen, in 1486, and subsequently ordained a priest; but he had no taste for the monastery, preferring instead a life of study, travel, and independence.

An opportunity for an escape from Stein came when Erasmus was appointed secretary to Henri de Bergues, Bishop of Cambray. After a brief time in the bishop's service, Erasmus entered the University of Paris. Since the bishop had supplied him with but scanty means, Erasmus was forced to augment his income by teaching. One of his students, Lord Mountjoy, brought Erasmus to England, where he resided from 1497 to 1500; while continuing his studies at Oxford, Erasmus made the acquaintance of several of England's leading scholars, including John Colet, William Grocyn, and Thomas Linacre. After leaving England, Erasmus traveled about Europe for the next several years, revisiting England in 1506, when he met Thomas More, and realizing a long-cherished dream to see Italy, where he lived from 1506 to 1509, earning his income first as tutor to the children of the physician of King Henry VII of England and later as tutor to Alexander Stuart, son of King James IV of Scotland.

In 1509, Erasmus returned to England as the guest of Thomas More. It was at More's house in London that Erasmus completed *The Praise of Folly* (*Encomium Moriae*), which he had begun composing during his return from Italy. While Erasmus had not initially intended the work for publication, a copy found its way into the hands of the printers Badius at Paris, and came out in 1512.

The Praise of Folly caused such a sensation that it went through more than forty editions in Erasmus' lifetime. The work was written in the tradition of "fool literature" then popular in Europe. The fashion

had been set with Sebastian Brant's *Narrenschiff,* or *Ship of Fools,*
first published in 1497. The *Narrenschiff,* describing over a hundred
different kinds of fools with blunt realism, was translated into Latin,
French, and English, and fostered a host of adaptations which were
circulating at the time Erasmus began to write *The Praise of Folly.*
This genre proved congenial to the classical scholar Erasmus, as it
appropriated several features of Roman satire, which combined humor
with pointed attacks on human weaknesses and excesses. Erasmus'
principal targets, in *The Praise of Folly,* were the church and the
papacy, although he by no means neglected princes, fortune-hunters,
pedantic schoolmasters, and the superstitious. So great was Erasmus'
aversion to the outrages of contemporary Catholicism that it gave
rise to the adage that "Erasmus laid the [reformist] egg and Luther
hatched it." Nevertheless, the gentle humanist of Rotterdam would
find equally repellent Luther's vulgar pamphlets and what he saw
as the violence of the new Protestant preachers.

Following the completion of *The Praise of Folly,* Erasmus moved
to Cambridge, where he was appointed Regius Professor of Greek
at Queen's College. After leaving England in 1513 (although he would
visit that nation thereafter), Erasmus refused all further academic posts
and offers of patronage for a life of precarious freedom paid for
by the sales of his writings and cash gifts from wealthy ecclesiastics.

In 1520, Erasmus settled in Basle, where he became the general
editor at Johann Froben's press. Froben's enterprise and Erasmus'
editorial skills raised the level of the press, for the next seven years,
to the best in Europe. At Basle, Erasmus published his editions of
the Church Fathers and a New Testament in Greek, with a Latin
translation.

After Froben's death in 1527, Erasmus left Basle, disturbed over
the zealotry of the religious movements then taking place all over
Switzerland. He lived for a time in Freiburg but returned to Basle,
where he died, at age sixty-nine, on July 12, 1536.

Erasmus' other works include *Adagia* (1500), *Enchiridion militis
Christiani* (1503), *Novum instrumentum* (1516), and *Colloquia famil-
iaria* (1518).

ERASMUS OF ROTTERDAM

To his Friend

THOMAS MORE, Health:

AS I was coming a while since out of Italy for England, that I might not waste all that time I was to sit on Horsback in foolish and illiterate Fables, I chose rather one while to revolve with my self something of our common Studies, and other while to enjoy the remembrance of my Friends, of whom I left here some no lesse learned than pleasant. Amongst these you, my More, came first in my mind, whose memory, though absent your self, gives me such delight in my absence, as when present with you I ever found in your company; than which, let me perish if in all my life I ever met with any thing more delectable. And therefore, being satisfy'd that something was to be done, and that that time was no wise proper for any serious matter, I resolv'd to make some sport with The Praise of Folly. But who the Devil put that in thy head? you'l say. The first thing was your sirname of More, which comes so near the word *Moriæ* (Folly) as you are far from the thing. And that you are so, all the world will clear you. In the next place, I conceiv'd this exercise of wit would not be least approv'd by you; inasmuch as you are wont to be delighted with such kind of mirth, that is to say, neither unlearned, if I am not mistaken, nor altogether insipid, and in the whole course of your life have play'd the part of a Democritus. And though such is the excellence of your Judgement that 'twas ever contrary to that of the people's, yet such is your incredible affability and sweetness of temper that you both can and delight to carry your self to all men a man of all hours. Wherefore you will not only with good will accept this small Declamation, but take upon you the defence of 't, forasmuch as being dedicated to you, it is now no longer mine but yours. But perhaps there will not be wanting some wranglers that may cavil and charge me, partly that these toyes are lighter than may become a Divine, and partly more biting than may beseem the modesty of a Christian, and consequently exclaim that I resemble the Ancient Comedy, or another Lucian, and snarle at every thing. But I would have them whom the lightness or foolery of the Argument may offend, to consider that mine is not the first of this kind, but the same thing that has been often practis'd even by great Authors : when Homer, so many Ages since, did the like with the battel of Frogs and Mice ; Virgil, with the Gnat, and Puddings ; Ovid, with the Nut ; when Polycrates, and his Corrector Isocrates, extol'd Tyranny ; Glauco, Injustice ; Favorinus, Deformity, and the quartan Ague ; Synescius, Baldness ; Lucian, the Fly, and Flattery ; when Seneca made such sport with Claudius's Canonizations ; Plutarch, with his Dialogue between Ulysses and Gryllus ; Lucian and Apuleius, with the Asse ; and some other, I know not who, with the Hog that made his last Will and Testament, of which also, even S. Jerome makes mention. And therefore if they please, let 'em suppose I play'd at Tables for my diversion, or if they had rather have it so, that I rod on

a Hobby-horse. For what injustice is it, that
when we allow every course of life its Recrea-
tion, that Study only should have none? especially when such toyes are not without their
serious matter, and foolery is so handled that
the Reader that is not altogether thick-skull'd
may reap more benefit from 't than from some
men's crabbish and specious Arguments. As
when one, with long study and great pains,
patches many pieces together on the praise of
Rhetorick or Philosophy; another makes a
Panegyrick to a Prince; another encourages
him to a War against the Turks; another tells
you what will become of the world after himself
is dead; and another finds out some new device
for the better ordering of Goat's-wooll: for as
nothing is more trifling than to treat of serious
matters triflingly, so nothing carries a better
grace, than so to discourse of trifles as a man
may seem to have intended them least. For
my own part, let other men judge of what I
have written; though yet, unlesse an over-
weening opinion of my self may have made me
blind in my own cause, I have prais'd Folly,
but not altogether foolishly. And now to say

somewhat to that other cavil, of biting. This liberty was ever permitted to all men's wits, to make their smart witty reflections on the common errors of mankind, and that too without offence, as long as this liberty does not run into licentiousness; which makes me the more admire the tender ears of the men of this age, that can away with solemn Titles. Nay, you'l meet with some so preposterously religious, that they will sooner endure the broadest scoffs even against Christ himself, than hear the Pope or a Prince be toucht in the least, especially if it be any thing that concerns their profit; whereas he that so taxes the lives of men, without naming any one in particular, whither, I pray, may he be said to bite, or rather to teach and admonish? Or otherwise, I beseech ye, under how many notions do I tax my self? Besides, he that spares no sort of men cannot be said to be angry with any one in particular, but the vices of all. And therefore, if there shall happen to be any one that shall say he is hit, he will but discover either his guilt or fear. Saint Jerome sported in this kind with more freedome and greater sharpnesse, not sparing sometimes men's

very name. But I, besides that I have wholly
avoided it, I have so moderated my stile, that
the understanding Reader will easily perceive
my endeavours herein were rather to make
mirth than bite. Nor have I, after the Example
of Juvenal, raked up that forgotten sink of filth
and ribaldry, but laid before you things rather
ridiculous than dishonest. And now, if there
be any one that is yet dissatisfied, let him at
least remember that it is no dishonour to be
discommended by Folly; and having brought
her in speaking, it was but fit that I kept up the
character of the person. But why do I run over
these things to you, a person so excellent an
Advocate that no man better defends his Client,
though the cause many times be none of the
best ? Farewell, my best disputant More, and
stoutly defend your Moriæ.

From the Country,
the 5th of the Ides of June.

MORIÆ ENCOMIUM

OR

THE PRAISE OF FOLLY

An Oration, of feigned matter, spoken by Folly in her own Person

AT what rate soever the World talks of me
(for I am not ignorant what an ill report
Folly hath got, even amongst the most Foolish),
yet that I am that She, that onely She, whose
Deity recreates both gods and men, even this
is a sufficient Argument, that I no sooner stept
up to speak to this full Assembly, than all your
faces put on a kind of new and unwonted
pleasantness. So suddenly have you clear'd
your brows, and with so frolique and hearty
a laughter given me your applause, that in troth,
as many of you as I behold on every side of me,
seem to me no less than Homer's gods drunk
with Nectar and Nepenthe; whereas before,

ye sat as lumpish and pensive as if ye had come
[1] from consulting an Oracle. And as it usually
happens when the Sun begins to shew his
Beams, or when after a sharp Winter the Spring
breathes afresh on the Earth, all things imme-
diately get a new face, new colour, and recover
as it were a certain kind of youth again : in like
manner, by but beholding me, ye have in an
instant gotten another kind of Countenance ;
and so what the otherwise great Rhetoricians
with their tedious and long-studied Orations
can hardly effect, to wit, to remove the trouble
of the Mind, I have done it at once, with my
single look.

But if ye ask me why I appear before you in
this strange dress, be pleas'd to lend me your
ears, and I'le tell you ; not those ears, I mean,
ye carry to Church, but abroad with ye, such
as ye are wont to prick up to Jugglers, Fools and
Buffons, and such as our Friend Midas once gave
to Pan. For I am dispos'd awhile to play the
Sophister with ye ; not of their sort who
nowadays buzle Young-men's heads with certain
empty notions and curious trifles, yet teach them

[1] e Trophonii specu.

nothing but a more than Womanish obstinacy of scolding : but I'le imitate those Antients, who, that they might the better avoid that infamous appellation of *Sophi* or *Wise*, chose rather to be call'd Sophisters. Their business was to celebrate the Praises of the gods and valiant men. And the like Encomium shall ye hear from me, but neither of Hercules nor Solon, but mine own dear Self, that is to say, Folly. Nor do I esteem those Wise-men a rush, that call it a foolish and insolent thing to praise one's self. Be it as foolish as they would make it, so they confess it proper : and what can be more, than that Folly be her own Trumpet ? For who can set me out better than my self, unless perhaps I could be better known to another than to my self? Though yet I think it somewhat more modest than the general practice of our Nobles and Wise men, who, throwing away all shame, hire some flattering Orator or Lying Poet, from whose mouth they may hear their praises, that is to say meer lyes ; and yet, com-posing themselves with a seeming modesty, spread out their Peacock's plumes and erect their Crests, whilst this impudent Flatterer

equals a man of nothing to the gods, and pro-
poses him as an absolute pattern of all Virtue
that's wholly a stranger to 't, sets out a pittiful
Jay in other's Feathers, washes the Blackmoor
white, and lastly [1] swells a Gnat to an Elephant.
In short, I will follow that old Proverb that says,
' He may lawfully praise himself that lives far
from Neighbours.' Though, by the way, I cannot
but wonder at the ingratitude, shall I say, or
negligence of Men, who, notwithstanding they
honour me in the first place and are willing
enough to confess my bounty, yet not one of
them for these so many ages has there been, who
in some thankful Oration has set out the praises
of Folly; when yet there has not wanted them,
whose elaborate endeavours have extol'd Tyrants,
Agues, Flyes, Baldness and such other Pests of
Nature, to their own loss of both time and sleep.
And now ye shall hear from me a plain extem-
porary speech, but so much the truer.   Nor
would I have ye think it like the rest of Orators,
made for the Ostentation of Wit; for these,
as ye know, when they have been beating their
heads some thirty years about an Oration, and

---

[1] ex musca elephantem.

at last perhaps produce somewhat that was never their own, shall yet swear they compos'd it in three dayes, and that too for diversion : whereas I ever lik't it best to speak [1] whatever came first out.

But let none of ye expect from me, that after the manner of Rhetoricians I should go about to Define what I am, much less use any Division ; for I hold it equally unlucky to circumscribe her whose Deity is universal, or make the least Division in that Worship about which every thing is so generally agree'd. Or to what purpose, think ye, should I describe my self, when I am here present before ye, and ye behold me speaking ? For I am, as ye see, that true and onely giver of wealth, whom the Greeks call Μωρία, the Latines *Stultitia*, and our plain English *Folly*. Or what need was there to have said so much, as if my very looks were not sufficient to inform ye who I am ? Or as if any man, mistaking me for Wisedome, could not at first sight convince himself by my face, the true index of my mind ? I am no Counterfeit, nor do I carry one thing in my looks and another in

[1] quicquid in buccam venerit.

my breast. No, I am in every respect so like
my self, that neither can they dissemble me, who
arrogate to themselves the appearance and title
of Wisemen, and walk [1] like Asses in Scarlet-
hoods ; though after all their hypocrisie Midas's
ears will discover their Master. A most ingrateful
generation of men, that, when they are wholly
given up to my Party, are yet publickly asham'd
of the name, as taking it for a reproach ; for
which cause, since in truth they are Μωρότατοι,
Fools, and yet would appear to the World to
be Wisemen and Thales's, wee'll ev'n call 'em
Μωροσόφους, Wise-fools.

Nor will it be amiss also to imitate the Rhetoricians of our times, who think themselves in a
manner Gods, if like Horse-leeches they can but
appear to be double-tongu'd ; and believe they
have done a mighty act if in their Latin Orations
they can but shuffle-in some ends of Greek,
like Mosaick-work, though altogether by head
and shoulders and less to the purpose. And if
they want hard words, they run over some
Worm-eaten Manuscript, and pick out half
a Dozen of the most old and absolete to con-

---

[1] in purpura simiae.

found their Reader, believing, no doubt, that they that understand their meaning will like it the better, and they that do not, will admire it the more by how much the lesse they understand it. Nor is this way of ours of admiring what seems most Forreign without it's particular grace; for if there happen to be any more ambitious than others, they may give their applause with a smile, and, like the Asse, [1] shake their ears, that they may be thought to understand more than the rest of their neighbours.

But to come to the purpose : I have giv'n ye my name; but what Epithet shall I adde? What but that of the most Foolish? For by what properer name can so great a goddess as Folly be known to her Disciples? And because it is not alike known to all from what stock I am sprung, with the Muses' good leave I'le do my endeavour to satisfie you. But yet neither the first Chaos, Orcus, Saturn, or Japhet, nor any of those thred-bare, musty Gods, were my Father, but Plutus, Riches; that only he, that is, in spight of Hesiod, Homer, nay and

[1] τὰ ὦτα κινῶσι.

Jupiter himself, *Divum Pater atque Hominum Rex*, the Father of Gods and Men ; at whose single beck, as heretofore, so at present, all things Sacred and Prophane are turn'd topsie turvy.   According to whose Pleasure War, Peace, Empire, Counsels, Judgements, Assemblies, Wedlocks, Bargains, Leagues, Laws, Arts, all things Light or Serious—I want breath—in short, all the publick and private business of mankind, is govern'd ; without whose help all that Herd of Gods of the Poets' making, and those few of the better sort of the rest, either would not be at all, or if they were, they would be but [1] such as live at home and keep a poor house to themselves.   And to whomsoever hee's an Enemy, 'tis not Pallas her self that can befriend him : as on the contrary he whom he favours may lead Jupiter and his Thunder in a string.   This is my father [2] and in him I glory. Nor did he produce me from his brain, as Jupiter that sowre and ill-look'd Pallas ; but [3] of that lovely Nymph call'd Youth, the most beautiful and galliard of all the rest.   Nor was

[1] οἰκόσιτοι.   [2] Hujus me glorior esse.
[3] ex Neotete Nympha.

I, like that limping Black-smith, begot in the sad and irksome bonds of Matrimony. Yet, mistake me not, 'twas not that blind and decrepit Plutus in Aristophanes that got me, but such as he was in his full strength and pride of youth; and not that onely, but at such a time when he had been well heated with Nectar, of which he had, at one of the Banquets of the Gods, taken a dose extraordinary.

And as to the place of my birth, forasmuch as nowadays that is look'd upon as a main point of Nobility, it was neither, like Apollo's, in the floating Delos, nor Venus-like on the rolling Sea, nor in any of blind Homer's as blind Caves: but in the fortunate Islands, where [1] all things grew without plowing or sowing; where neither Labour, nor Old-age, nor Disease, was ever heard of; and in whose fields neither Daffadil, Mallows, Onyons, Beans, and such contemptible things would ever grow; but, on the contrary, Rue, Angelica, Buglosse, Marjoram, Trefoiles, Roses, Violets, Lillies, and all the Gardens of Adonis, invite both your sight and your smelling. And being thus born, I did not begin the world,

[1] —sponte sua per se dabat omnia tellus.

as other Children are wont, with crying; but
streight perch'd up and smil'd on my mother.
Nor do I envy to the great Jupiter the Goat,
his Nurse, forasmuch as I was suckled by two
jolly Nymphs, to wit, Drunkenness, the daughter
of Bacchus, and Ignorance, of Pan. And as for
such my companions and followers as ye perceive
about me, if you have a mind to know who they
are, ye are not like to be the wiser for me, unlesse
it be in Greek: This here, which you observe
with that proud cast of her eye, is Φιλαυτία,
Self-love; She with the smiling countenance,
that is ever and anon clapping her hands, is
Κολακία, Flattery; She that looks as if she
were half asleep, is Λήθη, Oblivion; She that
sits leaning on both Elbows with her hands
clutch'd together, is Μισοπονία, Laziness; She
with the Garland on her head, and that smells
so strong of perfumes, is Ἡδονὴ, Pleasure; She
with those staring eyes, moving here and there,
is Ἀνοία, Madness; She with the smooth Skin
and full pamper'd body is Τρυφὴ, Wantonness;
and, as to the two Gods that ye see with them,
the one is Κῶμος, Intemperance, the other
Νήγρετος ὕπνος, Dead Sleep. These, I say, are

my houshold Servants, and by their faithful Counsels I have subjected all things to my Dominion, and erected an empire over Emperors themselves. Thus have ye had my Lineage, Education, and Companions.

And now, lest I may seem to have taken upon me the name of Goddess without cause, you shall in the next place understand how far my Deity extends, and what advantage by 't I have brought both to Gods and Men. For, if it was not unwisely said by some body, that this only is to be a God, To help Men; and if they are deservedly enroll'd among the Gods that first brought in Corn and Wine and such other things as are for the common good of mankind, why am not I of right the ἄλφα, or first, of all the gods? who being but one, yet bestow all things on all men. For first, What is more sweet or more precious than Life? And yet from whom can it more properly be said to come than from me? For neither [1] the Crab-favour'd Pallas's spear, nor [2] the Cloud-gathering Jupiter's Shield, either beget, or propagate mankind; But even he himself, the

---

[1] ὀβριμοπάτρης Palladis hasta.   [2] νεφεληγερέτου Jovis ægis.

Father of Gods, and King of Men [1] at whose
very beck the Heavens shake, must lay-by his
forked thunder, and those looks wherewith
he conquer'd the Gyants, and with which at
pleasure he frights the rest of the Gods, and like
a Common Stage-player put on a Disguise, as
often as he goes about that, which now and then
he do's, that is to say [2] the getting of children :
And the Stoicks too, that conceive themselves
next to the Gods, yet shew me one of them, nay
the veryest Bygot of the Sect, and if he do
not put off his beard, the badge of Wisdom,
though yet it be no more than what is common
with him and Goats ; yet at least he must lay-by
his supercilious Gravity, smooth his forehead,
shake off his rigid Principles, and for some time
commit an act of folly and dotage. In fine, that
Wiseman who ever he be, if he intends to have
Children must have recourse to me. But tell
me, I beseech ye, What Man is that would
submit his neck to the Noose of Wedlock, if as
Wisemen should, he did but first truly weigh the
inconvenience of the thing ?   Or what Woman
is there would ever go to 't did she seriously

---

[1] qui nutu tremefactat Olympum.   [2] παιδοποιεῖν.

consider either the peril of Child-bearing, or
the trouble of bringing them up? So then,
if ye owe your beings to Wedlock, ye owe that
Wedlock to this my follower, Madness; and
what ye owe to me I have already told ye.
Again, she that has but once try'd what it is,
would she, do ye think, make a second venture,
if it were not for my other Companion, Oblivion? Nay, even Venus her self, notwithstanding
what ever Lucretius has said, would not deny
but that all her vertue were lame and fruitless
without the help of my Deity. For out of that
little, odd, ridiculous May-game came the
supercilious Philosophers, in whose room have
succeeded a kind of people the world calls Monks,
Cardinals, Priests, and the most holy Popes.
And Lastly, all that Rabble of the Poets'-Gods,
with which Heaven is so thwack't and throng'd,
that though it be of so vast an extent, they are
hardly able to croud one by another.

But I think it a small matter that ye thus owe
your beginning of life to me, unless I also shew
you that whatever benefit you receive in the
progress of it is of my gift likewise. For what
other is this? Can that be call'd life where ye

take away pleasure? Oh! Do ye like what
I say? I knew none of you could have so little
Wit, or so much folly, or Wisdom rather, as to
be of any other opinion. For even the Stoicks
themselves, that so severely cry'd down pleasure,
did but handsomly dissemble, and rail'd against
it to the common People, to no other end
but that having discourag'd them from it, they
might the more plentifully enjoy it themselves.
But tell me, by Jupiter, what part of man's life
is that that is not sad, crabbed, unpleasant,
insipid, troublesome, unless it be seasoned with
Pleasure, that is to say, Folly? For the proof
of which the never-sufficiently prais'd Sophocles,
in that his happy Elogy of us [1] ' To know nothing
is the onely happiness', might be Authority
enough, but that I intend to take every particular by it's self.

And first, Who knows not but a man's Infancy
is the merriest part of life to himself, and most
acceptable to others? For what is that in them
which we kiss, embrace, cherish, nay Enemies
succour, but this witchcraft of Folly, which
wise Nature did of purpose give them into the

---

[1] Ἐν τῷ φρονεῖν γὰρ μηδὲν ἥδιστος βίος.

world with them, that they might the more pleasantly passe-over the toil of Education, and as it were flatter the care and diligence of their Nurses. And then for Youth, which is in such reputation everywhere, how do all men favour it, study to advance it and lend it their helping hand? And whence, I pray, all this Grace? Whence but from me? by whose kindness, as it understands as little as may be, it is also for that reason the higher priviledged from exceptions; and I am mistaken if, when it is grown up and by experience and discipline brought to savour something like Man, if in the same instant that beauty does not fade, it's liveliness decay, it's pleasantness grow flat, and it's briskness fail. And by how much the further it runs from me, by so much the less it lives, till it comes to [1] the burthen of Old age, not onely hateful to others, but to it self also. Which also were altogether insupportable did not I pitty it's condition, in being present with it, and, as the Poets'-gods were wont to assist such as were dying with some pleasant Metamorphωsis, help their decrepitness as much as

[1] molesta senectus.

in me lies by bringing them back to a second childhood, from whence they are not improperly called [1] Twice-Children. Which, if ye ask me how I do it, I shall not be shy in the point. I bring them to our River Lethe (for it's spring-head rises in the Fortunate Islands, and that other of Hell is but a Brook in comparison), from which, as soon as they have drunk down a long forgetfulness, they wash away by degrees the perplexity of their minds, and so wax young again.

But perhaps you'll say, They are foolish and doting. Admit it ; 'tis the very essence of Child-hood ; as if to be such were not to be a fool, or that that condition had any thing pleasant in it, but that it understood nothing. For who would not look upon that Child as a Prodigy that should have as much Wisdome as a Man ?—according to that common Proverb, [2] ' I do not like a Child that is a Man too soon.' Or who would endure a Converse or Friendship with that Old-man, who to so large an experience of things, had joyn'd an equal strength of mind and sharpness of judgement ?   And therefore

---

[1] Παλίμπαιδας.

[2] Odi puerulum praecoci sapientia.

for this reason it is that Old-age dotes ; and that it does so, it is beholding to me. Yet, not withstanding, is this dotard exempt from all those cares that distract a Wise man ; he is not the less pot-Companion, nor is he sensible of that burden of life, which the more manly Age finds enough to do to stand upright under 't. And sometimes too, like Plautus's Old-man, he returns to his three Letters, A.M.O., the most unhappy of all things living, if he rightly understood what he did in 't. And yet, so much do I befriend him, that I make him well receiv'd of his friends, and no unpleasant Companion ; for as much as, according to Homer, [1] Nestor's discourse was pleasanter than Honey, whereas Achilles's was both bitter and malicious ; and that of Old-men, as he has it in another place, florid. In which respect, also, they have this advantage of children, in that they want the onely pleasure of t' others life, we'll suppose it pratling. Adde to this that old men are more eagerly delighted with children, and they, again, with Old-men. [2] ' Like to like ', quoth the Divel

[1] Melle dulcior fluit oratio.
[2] ὅμοιον ἄγει θεὸς ὡς τὸν ὅμοιον.

to the Collier. For what difference between them, but that the one has more wrinckles and years upon his head than the other? Otherwise, the brightness of their hair, toothless mouth, weakness of body, love of Milk, broken speech, chatting, toying, forgetfulness, inadvertency, and briefly, all other their actions, agree in every thing. And by how much the nearer they approach to this Old-age, by so much they grow backward into the likeness of Children, until like them they pass from life to death, without any weariness of the one, or sense of t' other.

And now, let him that will compare the benefits they receive by me, with the Metamorphoses of the Gods; of whom, I shall not mention what they have done in their pettish humours, but where they have been most favourable : turning one into a Tree, another into a Bird, a third into a Grashopper, Serpent, or the like. As if there were any difference between perishing, and being another thing ! But I restore the same man to the best and happiest part of his life. And if Men would but refrain from all commerce with Wisdom, and give up themselves to be govern'd by me, they should never know what it were to be old, but solace themselves with a perpetual youth. Do but observe our grim Philosophers that are perpetually beating their brains on knotty Subjects, and for the most part you'll find 'em grown old before they are scarce young. And whence is it, but that their continual and restless thoughts insensibly prey upon their spirits, and dry up their Radical Moisture? Whereas, on the contrary, my fat fools are as plump and round as a Westphalian Hogg, and never sensible of old age, unless perhaps, as sometimes it rarely happens, they come to be infected with Wisdom ; so hard a thing it is for a man to be happy in all things. And to this purpose is that no small testimony of the Proverb, that sayes, ' Folly is the onely thing that keeps Youth at a stay, and Old age afar off ; ' as it is verifi'd in the Braban-ders, of whom there goes this common saying, ' That Age, which is wont to render other Men wiser, makes them the greater Fools.' And yet there is scarce any Nation of a more jocund converse, or that is less sensible of the misery of Old age, than they are. And to these, as in

scituation, so for manner of living, come nearest
my friends the Hollanders. And why should
I not call them mine, since they are so diligent
observers of me that they are commonly call'd
by my name?—of which they are so far from
being asham'd, they rather pride themselves in 't.
Let the foolish world then be packing and
seek out Medeas, Circes, Venuses, Auroras and
I know not what other Fountains of restoring
Youth. I am sure I am the onely person that
both can, and have made it good. 'Tis I alone
that have that wonderful Juice with which
Memnon's daughter prolong'd the youth of her
Grandfather Tithon. I am that Venus by whose
favour Phaon became so young again that Sappho
fell in love with him. Mine are those Herbs,
if yet there be any such, mine those Charms,
and mine that Fountain, that not onely restores
departed Youth but, which is more desirable,
preserves it perpetual. And if ye all subscribe
to this Opinion, that nothing is better than
Youth, or more execrable than Age, I conceive
you cannot but see how much ye are indebted
to me, that have retain'd so great a good, and
shut out so great an evil.

But why do I altogether spend my breath in
speaking of Mortals? View Heaven round, and
let him that will, reproach me with my name,
if he find any one of the Gods that were not
stinking and contemptible, were he not made
acceptable by my Deity. Whence is it that
Bacchus is always a Stripling, and bushy-hair'd?
but because he is mad, and drunk, and spends
his life in Drinking, Dancing, Revels, and May-
games, not having so much as the least society
with Pallas. And lastly, he is so far from
desiring to be accounted wise, that he delights
to be worshipp'd with Sports and Gambals;
nor is he displeas'd with the Proverb that gave
him the sirname of Fool, [1] 'A greater Fool than
Bacchus'; which name of his was chang'd to
Morychus, for that sitting before the gates of
his Temple, the wanton Countrey people were
wont to bedaub him with new Wine and Figgs.
And of scoffs, what not, hath not the antient
Comedies thrown on him? O foolish God, say
they, and worthy to be born as thou wert
of thy Father's thigh! And yet, who had not
rather be thy Fool and Sot, alwayes merry, ever

[1] Morycho stultior.

young, and making sport for other people,
than either Homer's Jupiter, with his crooked
Councels, terrible to every one; or old Pan with
his Hubbubs; or smutty Vulcan half-cover'd
with Cinders; or even Pallas her self, so dreadful
with her Gorgon's Head and Spear and a
Countenance like Bul-beef? Why is Cupid
always Pourtrai'd like a Boy, but because he
is a very Wagg, and can neither do nor so much
as think of any thing sober? Why Venus ever
in her prime, but because of her affinity with me?
Witness that colour of her Hair, so resembling
my Father, from whence she is call'd [1] the
golden Venus; and lastly, ever laughing, if ye
give any credit to the Poets, or their followers
the Statuaries. What Deity did the Romans
ever more religiously adore than that of Flora,
the foundress of all pleasure? Nay, if ye should
but diligently search the lives of the most
sowre and morose of the Gods out of Homer and
the rest of the Poets, you would find 'em all but
so many pieces of Folly. And to what purpose
should I run over any of the other gods' tricks
when ye know enough of Jupiter's loose Loves?

[1] Venus aurea.

when that chast Diana shall so far forget her
Sexe as to be ever hunting and ready to perish
for Endymion? But I had rather they should
hear these things from Momus, from whom
heretofore they were wont to have their shares,
till in one of their angry humours they tumbled
him, together with Ate, Goddess of Mischief,
down headlong to the Earth, because his wisdom,
forsooth, unseasonably disturb'd their happiness.
Nor since that dares any mortal give him harbour,
though I must confess there wanted little but
that he had been receiv'd into the Courts of
Princes, had not my companion Flattery reign'd
in chief there, with whom and t'other there is
no more correspondence than between Lambs
and Wolves. From whence it is that the Gods
play the fool with the greater liberty and more
content to themselves, [1]'doing all things care-
lessly,' as says Father Homer, that is to say,
without any one to correct them. For what
ridiculous stuff is there which that stump of the
Fig-tree Priapus does not afford 'em? what Tricks
and Legerdemains with which Mercury does
not cloak his thefts? what buffonry that Vulcan

[1] ῥᾷον ἄγοντες.

is not guilty of, while one while with his polt-
foot, another with his smutcht muzzle, another
with his impertinencies, he makes sport for the
rest of the Gods ? As also that old Silenus with
his Countrey-dances, Polyphemus footing time
to his Cyclops hammers, the Nymphs with their
Jiggs, and Satyrs with their Anticks; whilst Pan
makes 'em all twitter with some coarse Ballad,
which yet they had rather hear than the Muses
themselves, and chiefly when they are well
whitled with Nectar. Besides, what should I
mention what these Gods do when they are half
drunk ? Now by my troth, so foolish that I my
self can hardly refrain laughter. But in these
matters 'twere better we remember'd Harpo-
crates, lest some Eves-dropping God or other
take us whispering that which Momus onely has
the priviledge of speaking at length.

And therefore, according to Homer's example,
I think it high time to leave the Gods to themselves, and look down a little on the Earth;
wherein likewise you'll find nothing frolick or
fortunate, that it ows not to me. So provident
has that great Parent of Mankind, Nature, been,
that there should not be any thing without it's

mixture, and as it were seasoning of Folly. For since according to the definition of the Stoicks, Wisdom is nothing else than to be govern'd by reason ; and on the contrary Folly, to be giv'n up to the will of our Passions ; that the life of man might not be altogether disconsolate and hard to away with, of how much more Passion than Reason has Jupiter compos'd us ? putting in, as one would say, [1] ' scarce half an ounce to a pound '. Besides, he has confin'd Reason to a narrow corner of the brain, and left all the rest of the body to our Passions ; as also set up, against this one, two as it were, masterless Tyrants—Anger, that possesseth the region of the heart, and consequently the very Fountain of life, the Heart it self; and Lust, that stretcheth its Empire every where. Against which double force how powerful Reason is, let common experience declare, inasmuch as she, which yet is all she can do, may call out to us till she be hoarse again, and tell us the Rules of Honesty and Vertue ; while they give up the Reins to their Governour, and make a hideous clamour, till at last being wearied, he suffer himself

[1] Semiunciam ad assem.

to be carried whither they please to hurry
him.

But forasmuch as such as are born to the
business of the world have some little sprinklings
of Reason more than the rest, yet that they may
the better manage it, even in this as well as in
other things, they call me to counsel; and I
give 'em such as is worthy of my self, to wit
That they take to 'em a wife—a silly thing,
God wot, and foolish, yet wanton and pleasant,
by which means the roughness of the Masculine
temper is season'd and sweeten'd by her folly.
For in that Plato seems to doubt under which
Genus he should put woman, to wit that of
rational Creatures or Brutes, he intended no
other in it than to shew the apparent folly of
the Sexe. For if perhaps any of them goes about
to be thought wiser than the rest, what else
does she do but play the fool twice, as if a man
should [1]' teach a Cow to dance ', [2]' a thing quite
against the hair '. For as it doubles the crime
if any one should put a disguise upon Nature,
or endeavour to bring her to that she will in
no wise bear, according to that Proverb of the

---

[1] Bovem ad ceroma.   [2] invita reluctanteque Minerva.

Greeks, [1] 'An Ape is an Ape, though clad in Scarlet '; so a woman is a woman still, that is to say foolish, let her put on what ever Vizard she please.

But, by the way, I hope that Sexe is not so foolish as to take offence at this, that I my self, being a woman, and Folly too, have attributed Folly to them. For if they weigh it right, they needs must acknowledg that they owe it to Folly that they are more fortunate than men. As first their Beauty, which, and that not without cause, they prefer before every thing, since by its means they exercise a Tyranny even upon Tyrants themselves ; otherwise, whence proceeds that sowre look, rough skin, bushy beard and such other things as speak plain Old age in a man, but from that Disease of Wisdom ? whereas women's Cheeks are ever plump and smooth, their Voice small, their Skin soft, as if they imitated a certain kind of perpetual Youth. Again, what greater thing do they wish in their whole lives, than that they may please the Men ? For to what other purpose are all those Dresses, Washes, Baths, Curlings, Slops, Perfumes, and

[1] Simia est simia, etiamsi purpura vestiatur.

those several little tricks of setting their Faces,
painting their Eye-brows, and smoothing their
Skins? And now tell me, what higher Letters
of Recommendation have they to men than this
Folly? For what is it they do not permit 'em
to do? and to what other purpose than that
of pleasure? wherein yet their folly is not the
least thing that pleaseth; which how true it
is, I think no one will deny, that does but consider with himself, what foolish Discourse and
odd Gambals pass between a man and his
woman, as oft as he has a mind to be gamesome?
And so I have shown ye whence the first and
chiefest delight of man's life springs.

But there are some, you'll say, and those too
none of the youngest, that have a greater
kindness for the Pot than the Petticoat, and
place their chiefest pleasure in good fellowship.
If there can be any great entertainment without
a woman at it, let others look to 't. This I am
sure, there was never any pleasant which Folly
gave not the relish to. Insomuch that if they
find no occasion of Laughter, they send for [1] ' one
that may make it ', or hire some Buffon flatterer,

---

[1] γελωτοποιὸν quempiam.

whose ridiculous discourse may put by the Gravity
of the company. For to what purpose were it
to clogg our Stomacks with Dainties, Junkets
and the like Stuff, unless our Eyes and Ears, nay
whole Mind, were likewise entertain'd with Jests,
Merriments and Laughter? But of these kind
of second Courses I am the onely Cook; though
yet those ordinary practises of our Feasts,
as choosing a King, throwing Dice, drinking
Healths, trouling it Round, dancing the Cushion
and the like, were not invented by the seven
Wise Men but my Self, and that too for the
common pleasure of Mankind. The nature of
all which things is such, that the more of Folly
they have, the more they conduce to Humane
Life, which, if it were unpleasant, did not deserve
the name of Life; and other than such it could
not well be, did not these kind of Diversions
wype away tediousnesse, nexte cosyn to the
other.

But perhaps there are some that neglect this
way of pleasure, and rest satisfi'd in the enjoy-
ment of their Friends, calling friendship the
most desirable of all things; more necessary
than either air, fire, or water; so delectable,

that he that shall take it out of the World had
as good put out the Sun ; and lastly so commendable, if yet that make any thing to the
matter, that neither the Philosophers themselves
doubted to reckon it among their chiefest good.
But what if I shew you that I am both [1] the
beginning and end of this so great good also ?
Nor shall I go about to prove it by Fallacies,
Sorites, Dilemmas, or other the like subtilties of
Logicians, [2] but after my blunt way, point out
the thing as clearly as 'twere with my finger.

And now tell me, if to wink, slip over, be blind
at, or deceiv'd in, the vices of our friends, nay,
to admire and esteem them for Virtues, be not
at least the next degree to folly ? What is it
when one kisses his Mistresses freckle Neck,
another the Wart on her Nose ? When a Father
shall swear his squint-ey'd Child is more lovely
than Venus ? What is this, I say, but meer
folly ? And so, perhaps you'l cry, it is ; and yet
'tis this onely that joyns friends together, and
continues them so joyn'd. I speak of ordinary
men, of whom none are born without their im-

---

[1] prora et puppis.
[2] pingui, quod aiunt, Minerva.

perfections, and happy is he that is prest with
the least : for among wise Princes there is either
no friendship at all, or if there be, 'tis unpleasant
and reserv'd, and that too but amongst a very
few, 'twere a crime to say none. For that the
greatest part of mankind are fools, nay there
is not any one that dotes not in many things ;
and friendship, you know, is seldome made but
amongst equalls. And yet if it should so happen
that there were a mutual good-will between
them, it is in no wise firm nor very long liv'd ;
that is to say, among such as are morose and more
circumspect than needs, as being Eagle-sighted
into his friends' faults, but so blear-ey'd to their
own that they take not the least notice of the
Wallet that hangs behind their own Shoulders.
Since then the nature of Man is such that there
is scarce any one to be found that is not subject
to many errors, add to this the great diversity of
minds and studies, so many slips, oversights and
chances of humane life, and how is it possible
there should be any true friendship between those
Argus's, so much as one hour, were it not for
that which the Greeks excellently call εὐήθειαν ?
and you may render by Folly or good Nature,

chuse you whether. But what? Is not the Author
and Parent of all our Love, Cupid, as blind as
a beetle? and as with him [1] all colours agree,
so from him is it that every one likes his own
Sweeter-kin best, though never so ugly, and [2] 'that
an old man dotes on his old wife, and a boy on his
girle'. These things are not onely done every
where but laught at too, yet as ridiculous as
they are, they make society pleasant, and, as it
were, glew it together.

And what has been said of Friendship may
more reasonably be presum'd of Matrimony,
which in truth is no other than an insepar-
able conjunction of life. Good God! What
Divorces, or what not worse than that, would
daily happen, were not the converse between
a man and his wife supported and cherished
by flattery, apishnesse, gentlenesse, ignorance,
dissembling, certain Retainers of mine also!
Whoop holiday! how few marriages should we
have, if the Husband should but through-examin
how many tricks his pretty little Mop of Modesty
has plaid before she was marry'd! And how

---

[1] τὰ μὴ καλὰ καλὰ πέφανται.

[2] ut cascus cascam et pupus pupam deamet.

fewer of them would hold together, did not most of the Wife's actions escape the Husband's knowledg through his neglect or sottishness! And for this also ye are beholding to me, by whose means it is that the Husband is pleasant to his Wife, the Wife to her Husband, and the house kept in quiet. A man is laught at, when seeing his Wife weeping he licks up her tears. But how much happier is it to be thus deceiv'd than by being troubled with jealousie, not onely to torment himself, but set all things in a hubbub!

In fine, I am so necessary to the making of all society and manner of life both delightful and lasting, that neither would the people long endure their Governors, nor the Servant his Master, nor the Master his Footman, nor the Scholar his Tutor, nor one friend another, nor the Wife her Husband, nor the Userer the Borrower, nor a Souldier his Commander, nor one Companion another, unlesse all of them had their interchangeable failings, one while flattering, other while prudently conniving, and generally sweetning one another with some small relish of Folly.

And now you'd think I had said all, but ye

shall hear yet greater things. Will he, I pray,
love any one that hates himself? Or ever agree
with another who is not at peace with himself?
Or beget pleasure in another that is troublesome
to himself? I think no one will say it that is not
more foolish than Folly. And yet, if ye should
exclude me, there 's no man but would be so
far from enduring another that he would stink
in his own nostrils, be nauseated with his own
actions, and himself become odious to himself;
forasmuch as Nature, in too many things rather
a Stepdame than a Parent to us, has imprinted
that evil in men, especially such as have least
judgment, that every one repents him of his
own condition and admires that of others.
Whence it comes to pass that all her gifts,
elegancy and graces corrupt and perish. For
what benefit is Beauty, the greatest blessing of
Heaven, if it be mixt with affectation? What
Youth, if corrupted with the severity of old
Age? Lastly, what is that in the whole business
of a man's life he can do with any grace to himself
or others—for it is not so much a thing of Art,
as the very life of every Action, that it be done
with a good meen—unless this my friend and

companion, Self-love, be present with it? Nor does she without cause supply me the place of a Sister, since her whole endeavours are to act my part every where. For what is more foolish than for a man to study nothing else than how to please himself? To make himself the object of his own admiration? And yet, what is there that is either delightful or taking, nay rather what not the contrary, that a man does against the hair? Take away this Salt of life, and the Orator may ev'n sit still with his Action, the Musitian with all his division will be able to please no man, the Player be hist off the Stage, the Poet and all his Muses ridiculous, the Painter with his Art contemptible, and the Physitian with all his Slip-slops go a begging. Lastly, thou wilt be taken [1] for an Ugly fellow instead of a Beautiful, for Old and Decrepit instead of Youthful, and a Beast instead of a Wise man, a Child instead of Eloquent, and instead of a well-bred man, a clown. So necessary a thing it is that every one flatter himself, and commend himself to himself before he can be commended by others.

[1] pro Nireo Thersites, pro Phaone Nestor, pro Minerva sus.

Lastly, since it is the chiefest point of happinesse [1] ' that a man is willing to be what he is ', you have further abridg'd in this my Self-love, that no man's asham'd of his own face, no man of his own wit, no man of his own parentage, no man of his own house, no man of his manner of living, nor any man of his own Country; so that a Highlander has no desire to change with an Italian, a Thracian with an Athenian, nor a Scythian for the fortunate Islands. O the singular care of Nature, that in so great a variety of things has made all equal! Where she has been sometime sparing of her gifts she has recompenc'd it with the more of self-Love; though here, I must confess, I speak foolishly, it being the greatest of all other her Gifts: to say nothing that no great action was ever attempted without my Motion, or Art brought to perfection without my help.

Is not War the very Root and Matter of all Fam'd Enterprises? And yet what more foolish than to undertake it for I know not what trifles, especially when both Parties are sure to lose more than they get by the bargain? For of

[1] Quod sis, esse velis.

those that are slain, [1] not a word of them ; and
for the rest, when both sides are close engag'd
[2] ' and the Trumpets make an ugly noise ', what
use of those Wise men, I pray, that are so exhaust
with study that their thin cold Blood has scarce
any spirits left ?   No, it must be those blunt
fat fellows, that by how much the more they
exceed in Courage, fall short in Understanding.
Unless perhaps one had rather chuse Demosthenes
for a Souldier, who, following the example of
Archilochius, threw away his Arms and betook
him to his Heels e're he had scarce seen his
Enemy ; as ill a Souldier, as happy an Orator.

But Counsel, you'll say, is not of least concern in matters of War.   In a General I grant
it ; but this thing of Warring is no part of
Philosophy, but manag'd by Parasites, Pandars,
Thieves, Cut-throats, Plow-men, Sots, Spend-
thrifts and such other Dregs of Mankind, not
Philosophers ; who how unapt they are even
for common converse, let Socrates, whom the
Oracle of Apollo, though not so wisely, judg'd
' the wisest of all men living ', be witness ;

---

[1] οὐδεὶς λόγος.   [2] et rauco crepuerunt cornua cantu.

who stepping up to speak somewhat, I know
not what, in publique, was forc'd to come down
again well laught at for his pains. Though yet
in this he was not altogether a fool, that he re-
fus'd the appellation of Wise, and returning it
back to the Oracle, deliver'd his opinion That
a wise man should abstain from medling with
publique business; unless perhaps he should have
rather admonisht us to beware of Wisdom if we
intended to be reckon'd among the number of
men, there being nothing but his Wisdom that
first accus'd and afterwards sentenc't him to the
drinking of his poison'd Cup. For while, as ye
find him in Aristophanes, Philosophying about
Clouds and Ideas, measuring how far a Flea
could leap, and admiring that so small a creature
as a Flye should make so great a buzze, he medled
not with any thing that concern'd common life.
But his Master being in danger of his head,
his Scholar Plato is at hand, to wit that famous
Patron, that being disturb'd with the noise
of the people, could not go through half his
first Sentence. What should I speak of Theo-
phrastus, who being about to make an Oration,
became as dumb as if he had met a Wolfe in

his way, which yet would have put courage in
a Man of War? Or Isocrates, that was so cow-
hearted that he durst never attempt it? Or
Tully, that great Founder of the Roman
Eloquence, that could never begin to speak
without an odd kind of trembling, like a Boy
that had got the Hick-cop; which Fabius interprets as an argument of a wise Oratour and one
that was sensible of what he was doing; and
while he sayes it, does he not plainly confess
that Wisdom is a great obstacle to the true
management of business? What would become
of 'em, think ye, were they to fight it out at
blows, that are so dead through fear, when the
Contest is only with empty words?

And next to these is cry'd up, forsooth, that
goodly sentence of Plato's: 'Happy is that
Commonwealth where a Philosopher is Prince,
or whose Prince is addicted to Philosophy'.
When yet if ye consult Historians, you'll find
no Princes more pestilent to the Commonwealth
than where the Empire has fall'n to some
smatterer in Philosophy or one given to Letters.
To the truth of which I think the Catoes give
sufficient credit; of whom the one was ever

disturbing the peace of the Commonwealth
with his hair-brain'd accusations ; the other,
while he too wisely vindicated its liberty, quite
overthrew it. Add to this the Bruti, Cassii,
nay Cicero himself, that was no less perni-
cious to the Commonwealth of Rome than
was Demosthenes to that of Athens. Besides
M. Antoninus (that I may give ye one instance
that there was once one good Emperour ; for
with much ado I can make it out) was become
burthensome and hated of his Subjects, upon
no other score but that he was so great a Philosopher. But admitting him good, he did the
Commonwealth more hurt in leaving behind
him such a Son as he did, than ever he did it
good by his own Government. For these kind
of Men that are so given up to the study of
Wisdome are generally most unfortunate, but
chiefly in their Children ; Nature, it seems, so
providently ordering it, lest this mischief of
Wisdome should spread farther among mankind.
For which reason 'tis manifest why Cicero's Son was
so degenerate, and that wise Socrates's Children,
as one has well observ'd, were more like their
Mother than their Father, that is to say, Fools.

However this were to be born with, if only as to publick Employments they were [1] ' Like a Sow upon a pair of organs ', were they any thing apter to discharge even the common Offices of Life. Invite a Wise man to a Feast and he'll spoil the company, either with Morose silence or troublesome Disputes. Take him out to Dance, and you'l swear [2] ' a Cow would have don 't better '. Bring him to the Theatre, and his very looks are enough to spoil all, till like Cato he take an occasion of withdrawing rather than put off his supercilious gravity. Let him fall into discourse, and [3] he shall make more sudden stops than if he had a Woolf before him. Let him buy, or sell, or in short go about any of those things without which there is no living in this world, and you 'l say this piece of Wisdom were rather a Stock than a Man, of so little use is he to himself, Country, or Friends ; and all because he is wholly ignorant of common things, and lives a course of life quite different from the people ; by which means 'tis impossible but that he

[1] Asini ad lyram.   [2] Camelus saltans.
[3] Lupus in fabula.

contract a popular odium, to wit, by reason
of the great diversity of their life and souls.
For what is there at all done among men that
is not full of Folly, and that too from fools and
to fools? Against which universal practice if
any single one shall dare to set up his throat, my
advice to him is, that following the example
of Timon, he retire into some desart and there
enjoy his wisdome to himself.

But, to return to my design, what power was
it that drew those stony, oken and wild people
into Cities, but flattery? For nothing else is
signify'd by Amphion and Orpheus's Harp.
What was it that, when the common people
of Rome were like to have destroy'd all by their
Mutiny, reduc'd them to Obedience? Was it
a Philosophical Oration? Least. But a ridiculous and childish Fable, of the Belly and the
rest of the Members. And as good success had
Themistocles in his of the Fox and Hedghog.
What wise man's Oration could ever have done
so much with the people as Sertorius's invention
of his white Hind? Or his ridiculous Emblem
of pulling off a Horse's Tail hair by hair? Or
as Lycurgus's his example of his two Whelps?

To say nothing of Minos and Numa, both which
rul'd their foolish multitudes with Fabulous
Inventions ; with which kind of Toyes that
great and powerful beast, the People, are led
any way. Again what City ever receiv'd Plato's
or Aristotle's Laws, or Socrates's Precepts?
But, on the contrary, what made the Decii
devote themselves to the Infernal Gods, or
Q. Curtius to leap into the Gulph, but an
empty vain glory, a most bewitching Sirene?
And yet 'tis strange it should be so condemn'd
by those wise Philosophers. For what is more
foolish, say they, than for a Suppliant Suiter
to flatter the people, to buy their favour with
gifts, to court the applauses of so many fools,
to please himself with their Acclamations, to
be carri'd on the people's shoulders as in triumph,
and have a brazen Statue in the Market place?
Add to this the adoption of Names and Sirnames;
those Divine Honours given to a man of no
Reputation, and the Deification of the most
wicked Tyrants with publicque Ceremonies ;
most foolish things, and such as one Democritus
is too little to laugh at. Who denies it? And
yet from this root sprang all the great Acts of

the Heroes, which the Pens of so many Eloquent
men have extoll'd to the Skies. In a word, this
Folly is that that lai'd the foundation of Cities;
and by it, Empire, Authority, Religion, Policy
and publique Actions are preserv'd; neither
is there any thing in Humane Life that is not
a kind of pastime of Folly.

But to speak of Arts, what set men's wits on
work to invent and transmit to Posterity so many
Famous, as they conceive, pieces of Learning,
but the thirst of Glory? With so much loss of
sleep, such pains and travel, have the most
foolish of men thought to purchase themselves
a kind of I know not what Fame, than which
nothing can be more vain. And yet notwithstanding, ye owe this advantage to Folly, and
which is the most delectable of all other, that
ye reap the benefit of other men's madness.

And now, having vindicated to my self the
praise of Fortitude and Industry, what think ye
if I do the same by that of Prudence? But some
will say, You may as well joyn Fire and Water.
It may be so. But yet I doubt not but to succeed
even in this also, if, as ye have done hitherto,
ye will but favour me with your attention.

And first, if Prudence depends upon Experience, to whom is the honour of that name more proper? To the Wiseman, who partly out of modesty and partly distrust of himself, attempts nothing; or the Fool, whom neither Modesty which he never had, nor Danger which he never considers, can discourage from any thing? The Wiseman has recourse to the Books of the Antients, and from thence picks nothing but subtilties of words. The Fool, in undertaking and venturing on the business of the world, gathers, if I mistake not, the true Prudence, such as Homer though blind may be said to have seen, when he said [1] 'The burnt child dreads the fire'. For there are two main obstacles to the knowledge of things, Modesty that casts a mist before the understanding, and Fear that, having fanci'd a danger, disswades us from the attempt. But from these Folly sufficiently frees us, and few there are that rightly understand of what great advantage it is to blush at nothing and attempt every thing.

But if ye had rather take Prudence for that that consists in the judgment of things, hear

[1] ῥεχθὲν δέ τε νήπιος ἔγνω.

me, I beseech ye, how far they are from it that
yet crack of the name.   For first 'tis evident
that all Humane things, like Alcibiades's Sileni
or rural Gods, carry a double face, but not the
least alike ; so that what at first sight seems
to be death, if you view it narrowly may prove
to be life ; and so the contrary.   What appears
beautiful may chance to be deform'd ; what
wealthy, a very begger ; what infamous, praise-
worthy ; what learned, a dunce ; what lusty,
feeble ; what jocund, sad ; what noble, base ;
what lucky, unfortunate ; what friendly, an
enemy ; and what healthful, noisome. In short,
view the inside of these Sileni, and you'll find
them quite other than what they appear ; which,
if perhaps it shall not seem so Philosophically
spoken, I'll make it plain to you [1] 'after my
blunt way '.   Who would not conceive a Prince
a great Lord and abundant in every thing ?
But yet being so ill furnisht with the gifts of
the mind, and ever thinking he shall never have
enough, he's the poorest of all men.   And
then for his mind so giv'n up to Vice, 'tis a
shame how it inslaves him.   I might in like

[1] pinguiore Minerva.

manner Philosophy of the rest; but let this one, for example's sake, be enough.

Yet why this? will some one say. Have patience, and I'll shew ye what I drive at. If any one seeing a Player acting his Part on a Stage, should go about to strip him of his disguise, and shew him to the people in his true Native Form, would he not, think ye, not onely spoil the whole design of the Play, but deserve himself to be pelted off with stones as a Phantastical Fool, and one out of his wits? But nothing is more common with them than such changes; the same person one while personating a Woman, and another while a Man; now a Youngster, and by and by a grim Seigniour; now a King, and presently a Peasant; now a God, and in a trice agen an ordinary Fellow. But to discover this were to spoil all, it being the onely thing that entertains the Eyes of the Spectators. And what is all this Life but a kind of Comedy, wherein men walk up and down in one another's Disguises, and Act their respective Parts, till the property-man brings 'em back to the Tyring House. And yet he often orders a different Dress, and makes him that came

but just now off in the Robes of a King, put
on the Raggs of a Begger.   Thus are all things
represented by Counterfeit, and yet without
this there were no living.

And here if any wise man, as it were dropt
from Heaven, should start up and cry, This
great thing, whom the World looks upon for
a God and I know not what, is not so much as
a Man, for that like a Beast he is led by his
Passions, but the worst of Slaves, inasmuch as
he gives himself up willingly to so many and such
detestable Masters.   Again if he should bid
a man that were bewailing the death of his
Father to laugh, for that he now began to live
by having got an Estate, without which Life
is but a kind of Death ; or call another that were
boasting of his Family, ill begotten or base,
because he is so far remov'd from Vertue that
is the only Fountain of Nobility ; and so of
the rest : what else would he get by 't but be
thought himself Mad and Frantick ?   For as
nothing is more foolish than preposterous
Wisdome, so nothing is more unadvised than a
froward unseasonable Prudence.   And such is
his that does not comply with the present

time [1] 'and order himself as the Market goes', but forgetting that Law of Feasts, [2] 'either drink or begon,' undertakes to disprove a common receiv'd Opinion. Whereas on the contrary 'tis the part of a truly Prudent man not to be wise beyond his Condition; but either to take no notice of what the world does, or run with it for company. But this is foolish, you'll say; nor shall I deny it, provided always ye be so civil on t' other side as to confess that this is to Act a Part in that World.

But, O ye Gods, [3] 'shall I speak or hold my tongue?' But why should I be silent in a thing that is more true than truth it self? However it might not be amiss perhaps in so great an Affair, to call forth the Muses from Helicon, since the Poets so often invoke 'em upon every foolish occasion. Be present then awhile, and assist me, ye Daughters of Jupiter, while I make it out that there is no way to that so much Fam'd Wisdome, nor access to that Fortress as they call it of Happiness, but under the Banner of

---

[1] et foro noluit uti. [2] ἤ πίθι ἤ ἄπιθι.

[3] Eloquar an sileam?

Folly. And first 'tis agreed of all hands that our passions belong to Folly; inasmuch as we judge a wise Man from a Fool by this, that the one is order'd by them, the other by Reason; and therefore the Stoicks remove from a wise man all disturbances of Mind as so many Diseases. But these Passions do not onely the Office of a Tutor to such as are making towards the Port of Wisdome, but are in every exercise of Vertue as it were Spurs and Incentives, nay and Encouragers to well doing : which though that great Stoick Seneca most strongly denys, and takes from a wise man all affections whatever, yet in doing that he leaves him not so much as a Man, but rather a new kind of God, that was never yet, nor ever like to be. Nay, to speak plainer, he sets up a stony Semblance of a Man, void of all Sense and common feeling of Humanity. And much good to them with this Wise Man of theirs; let them enjoy him to themselves, love him without Competitors, and live with him in Plato's Common-wealth, the Countrey of Ideas, or Tantalus's Orchards. For who would not shun and startle at such a man, as at some unnatural accident or Spirit ? A man

dead to all sense of Nature and common affections, and no more mov'd with Love or Pity
[1] than if he were a Flint or Rock; whose censure
nothing escapes; that commits no errors himself, but has a Lynx's eyes upon others; measures
every thing by an exact Line, and forgives
nothing; pleases himself with himself onely;
the onely Rich, the onely Wise, the onely Free
Man, and onely King; in brief, the onely man
that is every thing, but in his own single judgment onely; that cares not for the Friendship
of any man, being himself a friend to no man;
makes no doubt to make the Gods stoop to him,
and condemns and laughs at the whole Actions
of our Life? And yet such a Beast is this their
perfect Wise Man. But tell me pray, if the thing
were to be carri'd by most voices, what City
would chuse him for its Governour, or what
Army desire him for their General? What
Woman would have such a Husband, what
Good-fellow such a Guest, or what Servant
would either wish or endure such a Master?
Nay, who had not rather have one of the middle
sort of Fools, who, being a Fool himself, may

---

[1] Quam si dura silex aut stet Marpesia cautes.

the better know how to command or obey
Fools ; and who though he please his like, 'tis
yet the greater number ; one that is kind to
his Wife, merry among his Friends, a Boon
Companion, and easie to be liv'd with ; and
lastly one that thinks nothing of Humanity
should be a stranger to him ? But I am weary
of this Wise Man, and therefore I'll proceed to
some other advantages.

Go to then. Suppose a man in some lofty
high Tower, and that he could look round him,
as the Poets say Jupiter was now and then wont.
To how many misfortunes would he find the
life of man subject ? How miserable, to say no
worse, our Birth, how difficult our Education ;
to how many wrongs our Childhood expos'd,
to what pains our Youth ; how unsupportable
our Old-age, and grievous our unavoidable
Death ? as also what Troups of Diseases beset
us, how many Casualties hang over our Heads,
how many Troubles invade us, and how little
there is that is not steept in Gall ? to say nothing
of those evils one man brings upon another, as
Poverty, Imprisonment, Infamy, Dishonesty,
Racks, Snares, Treachery, Reproaches, Actions,

Deceipts—But I'm got into as endless a work as numbring the Sands—For what offences Mankind have deserv'd these things, or what angry God compell'd 'em to be born into such miseries, is not my present business. Yet he that shall diligently examine it with himself, would he not, think ye, approve the example of the Milesian Virgins, and kill himself? But who are they that for no other reason but that they were weary of life, have hastned their own Fate? were they not the next Neighbours to Wisdom? amongst whom, to say nothing of Diogenes, Xenocrates, Cato, Cassius, Brutus, that Wise Man Chiron, being offer'd Immortality, chose rather to dye than be troubled with the same thing always.

And now I think ye see what would become of the World if all men should be wise; to wit 'twere necessary we got another kind of Clay and some better Potter. But I, partly through ignorance, partly unadvisedness, and sometimes through forgetfulness of evil, do now and then so sprinkle pleasure with the hopes of good, and sweeten men up in their greatest misfortunes, that they are not willing to leave this life, even

then when according to the account of the
Destinys this life has left them ; and by how
much the less reason they have to live, by so
much the more they desire it ; so far are they
from being sensible of the least wearisomness of
life. Of my gift it is, that ye have so many old
Nestors every where, that have scarce left 'em
so much as the shape of a Man ; Stutterers,
Dotards, Toothless, Gray-hair'd, Bald ; or
rather, to use the words of Aristophanes, [1]'Nasty,
Crumpt, Miserable, Shrivel'd, Bald, Toothless,
and wanting their Baubles' : yet so delighted
with life and to be thought young, that one
dies his gray hairs ; another covers his baldness
with a Periwigg ; another gets a set of new
Teeth ; another falls desperately in love with
a young Wench, and keeps more flickering about
her than a young man would have been asham'd
of. For to see such an old crooked piece, with
one foot in the grave, to marrie a plump young
Wench, and that too without a portion, is so
common that men almost expect to be commended for 't. But the best sport of all is to

[1] ῥυπῶντας, κυφοὺς, ἀθλίους, ῥυσοὺς, μαδῶντας, νωδοὺς, καὶ
ψωλούς.

see our old Women, even dead with age, and
such skeletons one would think they h id stoln
out of their graves, and ever mumbling in their
mouths, [1] ' Life is sweet ' ; and as old as they
are, still catterwawling, daily plaistering their
face, scarce ever from the glasse, gossipping,
dancing, and writing Love-letters. These things
are laught at as foolish, as indeed they are ; yet
they please themselves, live merrily, swimme in
pleasure, and in a word are happy, by my
courtesie. But I would have them to whom
these things seem ridiculous, to consider with
themselves whether it be not better to live so
pleasant a life, in such kind of follies, than, as
the Proverb goes, ' To take a Halter and hang
themselves '. Besides though these things may
be subject to censure, it concerns not my fools
in the least, in as much as they take no notice
of it, or if they do, they easily neglect it. If a
stone fall upon a man's head, that's evil indeed ;
but dishonesty, infamy, villany, ill reports,
carrie no more hurt in them than a man is sensible
of ; and if a man have no sense of them, they are
no longer evils. What art thou the worse [2] if

[1] φῶς ἀγαθὸν.   [2] Si populus te sibilet, at tibi plaudas.

the people hisse at thee, so thou applaud thy
self? And that a man be able to do so, he must
ow it only to Folly.

But methinks I hear the Philosophers opposing
it, and saying 'tis a miserable thing for a man to
be foolish, to erre, mistake, and know nothing
truly. Nay rather, this is to be a man. And
why they should call it miserable, I see no
reason ; forasmuch as we are so born, so bred,
so instructed, nay, such is the common condition
of us all. And nothing can be call'd miserable
that suits with its kind, unless perhaps you'l
think a man such because he can neither flie
with Birds, nor walk on all four with Beasts,
and is not arm'd with Horns as a Bull. For
by the same reason he would call the Warlike
Horse unfortunate, because he understood not
Grammar, nor eat Chees-cakes ; and the Bull
miserable, because he'd make so ill a Wrestler.
And therefore, as a Horse that has no skill in
Grammar is not miserable, no more is man in
this respect, for that they agree with his Nature.
But again, the [1] Virtuosi may say that there
was particularly added to Man the knowledge

[1] Logodaedali.

of Sciences, by whose help he might recompence himself in Understanding for what Nature cut him short in other things. As if this had the least face of truth, that Nature, that was so sollicitously watchful in the production of Gnats, Herbs and Flowers, should have so slept when she made Man, that he should have need to be helpt by Sciences, which that old Devil Theuth, the evil Genius of mankind, first invented for his Destruction, and are so little conducing to happiness that they rather obstruct it ; to which purpose they are properly said to be first found out, as that wise King in Plato argues touching the invention of Letters.

Sciences therefore crept into the world with other the pests of mankind, from the same head from whence all other mischiefs spring ; wee'l suppose it Devils, for so the name imports when you call them Dæmons, that is to say, [1] Knowing. For that simple people of the golden Age, being wholly ignorant of every thing call'd Learning, liv'd only by the guidance and dictates of Nature ; for what use of Grammar, where every man spoke the same Language and had no

[1] δαήμονας.

further design than to understand one another?
What use of Logick, where there was no bickering
about the double-meaning words? What need
of Rhetorick, where there were no Law-suits?
Or to what purpose Laws, where there were no
ill manners? from which without doubt good
Laws first came. Besides, they were more
religious than with an impious curiosity to dive
into the secrets of Nature, the dimension of
Starrs, the motions, effects, and hidden causes
of things; as believing it a crime for any man
to attempt to be wise beyond his condition.
And as to the Inquiry of what was beyond
Heaven, that madness never came into their
heads. But the purity of the golden age declin-
ing by degrees, first, as I said before, Arts were
invented by the evil Genii; and yet but few,
and those too receiv'd by fewer. After that the
Chaldean Superstition and Greek newfangled-
ness, that had little to do, added I know not
how many more; meer torments of Wit, and
that so great that even Grammar alone is work
enough for any man for his whole life.

Though yet amongst these Sciences those
only are in esteem that come nearest to common

sense, that is to say, Folly. Divines are half
starv'd, Naturalists out of heart, Astrologers
laught at, and Logicians slighted; onely the
Physician [1] is worth all the rest. And amongst
them too, the more unlearned, impudent, or
unadvised he is, the more he is esteem'd, even
among Princes. For Physick, especially as it is
now profest by most men, is nothing but a
branch of Flattery, no less than Rhetorick.
Next them, the second place is given to our
Law-drivers, if not the first; whose Profession,
though I say it my self, most men laugh at as
the Ass of Philosophy; yet there's scarce any
business, either so great or small, but is manag'd
by these Asses. These purchase their great
Lordships, while in the mean time the Divine,
having run through the whole Body of Divinity,
sits gnawing a Raddish, and is in continual
Warfare with Lice and Fleas. As therefore those
Arts are best that have the nearest Affinity with
Folly, so are they most happy of all others
that have least commerce with Sciences, and
follow the guidance of Nature, who is in no
wise imperfect, unless perhaps we endeavor to

[1] πολλῶν ἀντάξιος ἄλλων.

leap over those bounds she has appointed to us. Nature hates all false-colouring, and is ever best where she is least adulterated with Art.

Go to then, don't ye find among the several kinds of living Creatures, that they thrive best that understand no more than what Nature taught them ? What is more prosperous or wonderful than the Bee ? And though they have not the same judgement of sense as other Bodies have, yet wherein hath Architecture gone beyond their building of Houses ? What Philosopher ever founded the like Republique ? Whereas the Horse, that comes so near man in understanding and is therefore so familiar with him, is also partaker of his misery. For while he thinks it a shame to lose the Race, it often happens that he cracks his wind ; and in the Battel, while he contends for Victory, he's cut down himself, and, together with his Rider, [1] 'lies biting the earth ' : not to mention those strong Bits, sharp Spurrs, close Stables, Arms, Blows, Rider, and briefly, all that slavery he willingly submits to, while, imitating those men of Valour, he so eagerly strives to be reveng'd of the Enemy.

[1] terram ore momordit.

Than which how much more were the life of
flies or birds to be wish'd for, who living by the
instinct of Nature look no further than the
present, if yet man would but let 'em alone in 't.
And if at any time they chance to be taken, and
being shut up in Cages endeavour to imitate
our speaking, 'tis strange how they degenerate
from their native gaiety. So much better in
every respect are the works of Nature than the
adulteries of Art.

 In like manner I can never sufficiently praise
that Pythagoras in a Dung-hill Cock, who being
but one had been yet every thing ; a Philosopher, a Man, a Woman, a King, a private man,
a Fish, a Horse, a Frog, and I believe too, a
Sponge ; and at last concluded that no Creature
was more miserable than man, for that all other
Creatures are content with those bounds that
Nature set them, onely Man endeavours to
exceed them. And again, among men he gives
the precedency not to the learned or the great,
but the Fool. Nor had that Gryllus less wit
than [1]Ulysses with his many counsels, who chose
rather to lie grunting in a Hog-sty than be

---

[1] πολύμητις Ὀδυσσεύς.

expos'd with t' other to so many hazzards. Nor
does Homer, that Father of trifles, dissent from
me; who not only call'd all men [1] 'wretched and
full of calamity', but often his great pattern of
Wisedom, Ulysses, [2] 'Miserable'; Paris, Ajax,
and Achilles no where. And why, I pray? but
that, like a cunning fellow and one that was
his craft's-master, he did nothing without the
advice of Pallas. In a word he was too wise, and
by that means ran wide of Nature. As therefore
amongst men they are least happy that study
Wisedom, as being in this twice-Fools, that when
they are born men they should yet so far forget
their condition as to affect the life of Gods;
and after the Example of the Gyants, with their
Philosophical gimcracks make a War upon
Nature : so they on the other side seem as little
miserable as is possible, who come nearest to
Beasts and never attempt any thing beyond
Man. Go to then, let's try how demonstrable
this is; not by Enthymems or the imperfect
Syllogisms of the Stoicks, but by plain, down-
right and ordinary Examples.

And now, by the immortal Gods! I think

---

[1] δειλοὺς καὶ μοχθηροὺς.   [2] δύστηνον.

nothing more happy than that generation of
men we commonly call fools, ideots, lack-wits
and dolts ; splendid Titles too, as I conceive
'em. I'le tell ye a thing, which at first perhaps
may seem foolish and absurd, yet nothing more
true. And first they are not afraid of death ;
no small evil, by Jupiter ! They are not tormented with the conscience of evil acts ; not
terrify'd with the fables of Ghosts, nor frighted
with Spirits and Goblins. They are not dis-
tracted with the fear of evils to come, nor the
hopes of future good. In short they are not
disturb'd with those thousand of cares to
which this life is subject. They are neither
modest, nor fearful, nor ambitious, nor envious,
nor love they any man. And lastly if they should
come nearer even to the very ignorance of
Brutes, they could not sin, for so hold the
Divines. And now tell me, thou wise fool, with
how many troublesome cares thy mind is con-
tinually perplext ; heap together all the discom-
modities of thy life, and then thou'lt be sensible
from how many evils I have delivered my Fools.
Add to this that they are not onely merry, play,
sing, and laugh themselves, but make mirth

where ever they come, a special priviledge it
seems the Gods have given 'em to refresh the
pensiveness of life. Whence it is, that whereas
the world is so differently affected one towards
another,—that all men indifferently admit
them as their companions, desire, feed, cherish,
embrace them, take their parts upon all occasions, and permit 'em without offence to do
or say what they list. And so little doth every
thing desire to hurt them, that even the very
Beasts, by a kind of natural instinct of their
innocence no doubt, pass by their injuries.
For of them it may be truly said that they are
consecrate to the Gods, and therefore and not
without cause do men have 'em in such esteem.
Whence is it else that they are in so great
request with Princes, that they can neither eat
nor drink, go any whither, or be an hour without
them? Nay, and in some degree they prefer
these Fools before their crabbish Wise-men,
whom yet they keep about them for State-sake.
Nor do I conceive the reason so difficult, or that
it should seem strange why they are prefer'd
before t' others, for that these wise men speak
to Princes about nothing but grave, serious

matters, and trusting to their own parts and learning do not fear sometimes [1]'to grate their tender ears with smart truths'; but fools fit 'em with that they most delight in, as jeasts, laughter, abuses of other men, wanton pastimes, and the like.

Again, take notice of this no contemptible blessing which Nature hath giv'n fools, that they are the only plain, honest men and such as speak truth. And what is more commendable than truth? for though that Proverb of Alcibiades in Plato attributes Truth to Drunkards and Children, yet the praise of it is particularly mine, even from the testimony of Euripides; amongst whose other things there is extant that his honourable saying concerning us, [2]'A fool speaks foolish things'. For whatever a fool has in his heart, he both shews it in his looks and expresses it in his discourse; while the wise men's are those two Tongues which the same Euripides mentions, whereof the one speaks truth, the other what they judge most seasonable for the occasion. These are they

---

[1] Auriculas teneras mordaci radere vero.

[2] μωρὰ γὰρ μωρὸς λέγει.

[1]'that turn black into white', blow hot and cold with the same breath, and carry a far different meaning in their Breast from what they feign with their Tongue. Yet in the midst of all their prosperity, Princes in this respect seem to me most unfortunate, because, having no one to tell them truth, they are forc't to receive flatterers for friends.

But, some one may say, the ears of Princes are strangers to truth, and for this reason they avoid those Wise men, because they fear lest some one more frank than the rest should dare to speak to them things rather true than pleasant; for so the matter is, that they don't much care for truth. And yet this is found by experience among my Fools, that not onely Truths but even open reproaches are heard with pleasure; so that the same thing which, if it came from a wise man's mouth might prove a Capital Crime, spoken by a Fool is receiv'd with delight. For Truth carries with it a certain peculiar Power of pleasing, if no Accident fall in to give occasion of offence; which faculty the Gods have given onely to Fools. And for the same reasons is it

[1] qui nigrum in candida vertunt.

that Women are so earnestly delighted with this
kind of Men, as being more propense by Nature
to Pleasure and Toyes. And whatsoever they
may happen to do with them, although sometimes it be of the seriousest, yet they turn it to
Jest and Laughter; as that Sexe was ever quick-
witted, especially to colour their own faults.

But to return to the happiness of Fools, who
when they have past over this life with a great deal
of Pleasantness, and without so much as the least
fear or sense of Death, they go straight forth
into the Elysian Field, to recreate their Pious
and Careless Souls with such Sports as they
us'd here. Let's proceed then, and compare the
condition of any of your Wise Men with that
of this Fool. Fancy to me now some example
of Wisdome you'd set up against him; one
that had spent his Childhood and Youth in
learning the Sciences; and lost the sweetest
part of his life in Watchings, Cares, Studies;
and for the remaining part of it never so much
as tasted the least of pleasure; ever sparing,
poor, sad, sowre, unjust and rigorous to himself,
and troublesome and hateful to others; broken
with Paleness, Leanness, Crasiness, sore Eyes,

and an Old-age and Death contracted before their time (though yet, what matter is it, when he dye that never liv'd ?) ; and such is the Picture of this great Wise Man.

And here again [1] do those Frogs of the Stoicks croak at me, and say that nothing is more miserable than Madness. But Folly is the next degree, if not the very thing. For what else is Madness than for a man to be out of his wits ? But to let 'em see how they are clean out of the way, with the Muses' good favour we'll take this Syllogism in pieces. Subtilly argu'd, I must confess, but as Socrates in Plato teaches us how by splitting one Venus and one Cupid to make two of either, in like manner should those Logicians have done, and distinguisht Madness from Madness, if at least they would be thought to be well in their wits themselves. For all Madness is not miserable, or Horace had never call'd his Poetical fury [2] a beloved Madness ; nor Plato plac'd the Raptures of Poets, Prophets and Lovers amongst the chiefest Blessings of this Life ; nor that Sybil in Virgil call'd Æneas's Travels Mad Labours. But there

---

[1] οἱ ἐκ τῆς στοᾶς βάτραχοι.   [2] amabilis insania.

are two sorts of Madness; the one that which
the revengeful Furies send privily from Hell,
as often as they let loose their Snakes, and put
into men's breasts either the desire of War,
or an insatiate thirst after Gold, or some dishonest Love, or Parricide, or Incest, or Sacriledge, or the like Plagues, or when they terrifie
some guilty soul with the Conscience of his
Crimes; the other, but nothing like this, that
which comes from me, and is of all other things
the most desirable; which happens as oft as
some pleasing dotage not onely clears the mind
of its troublesome cares, but renders it more
jocund. And this was that which, as a special
blessing of the Gods, Cicero, writing to his
friend Atticus, wisht to himself, that he might
be the less sensible of those miseries that then
hung over the Common-wealth.

Nor was that Grecian in Horace much wide
of it, who was so far mad that he would sit by
himself whole daies in the Theatre laughing
and clapping his hands, as if he had seen some
Tragedy acting, whereas in truth there was
nothing presented; yet in other things a man
well enough, pleasant among his Friends, kind

to his Wife, and so good a Master to his Servants, [1] that if they had broken the Seal of his
Bottle he would not have run mad for 't. But
at last, when by the care of his Friends and
Physick he was freed from his Distemper, and
become his own man again, he thus expostulates
with them: [2] 'Now, by Pollux, my Friends,
ye have rather kill'd than preserv'd me, in thus
forcing me from my pleasure'. By which you
see he lik'd it so well that he lost it against his
will. And trust me, I think they were the
madder o' th' two, and had the greater need of
Hellebore, that should offer to look upon so
pleasant a madness as an evil to be remov'd by
Physick; though yet I have not determin'd
whether every Distemper of the Sense or Understanding be to be call'd Madnesse.

For neither he that having weak eyes should
take a Mule for an Ass, nor he that should admire
an insipid Poem as excellent, would be presently
thought mad; but he that not onely erreth in
his senses, but is deceived also in his judgment,

[1] signo laeso non insanire lagenae.
[2]   Pol, me occidistis, amici,
Non servastis, ait, cui sic extorta voluptas.

and that too more than ordinary and upon all
occasions,—he, I must confess, would be thought
to come very near to it. As if any one hearing
an Ass bray should take it for excellent musick,
or a Begger conceive himself a King. And yet
this kind of madness, if, as it commonly happens,
it turn to pleasure, it brings a great delight not
onely to them that are possest with it, but to
those also that behold it ; though perhaps they
may not be altogether so mad as the other, for
the Species of this madness is much larger than
the people take it to be. For one mad man
laughs at another, and beget themselves a mutual
pleasure. Nor does it seldom happen, that he
that is the more mad, laughs at him that is lesse
mad. And in this every man is the more happy,
in how many respects the more he is mad ; and
if I were judge in the case, he should be rang'd in
that Classis of Folly that is peculiarly mine; which
in troth is so large and universal, that I scarce
know any one in all mankind that is wise at all
hours, or has not some tang or other of madness.

And to this Classis do they appertain that
sleight every thing in comparison of hunting,
and protest they take an unimaginable pleasure

to hear the yell of the Horns and the yelps of
the Hounds, and I believe could pick somewhat
extraordinary out of their very excrement.
And then what pleasure they take to see a Buck
or the like unlac'd ? Let ordinary fellows cut
up an Ox or a Weather, 'twere a crime to have
this done by any thing less than a Gentleman !
who with his Hat off, on his bare knees, and
a Cuttoe for that purpose (for every Sword or
Knife is not allowable), with a curious superstition and certain postures, layes open the several
parts in their respective order ; while they that
hemm him in admire it with silence, as some new
religious Ceremony, though perhaps they have
seen it an hundred times before. And if any
of 'em chance to get the least piece of 't, he
presently thinks himself no small Gentleman.
In all which they drive at nothing more than
to become Beasts themselves, while yet they
imagin they live the life of Princes.

And next these may be reckon'd those that have
such an itch of Building ; one while changing
Rounds into Squares, and presently again
[1] Squares into Rounds ; never knowing either

[1] quadrata rotundis.

measure or end, till at last, reduc'd to the utmost poverty, there remains not to them so much as a place where they may lay their head, or wherewith to fill their bellyes. And why all this? but that they may pass over a few years in feeding their foolish fancies.

And, in my opinion, next these may be reckon'd such as with their new inventions and occult arts undertake to change the forms of things, and hunt all about after a certain fifth Essence; Men so bewitcht with this present hope that it never repents them of their pains or expence, but are ever contriving how they may cheat themselves; till, having spent all, there is not enough left them to provide another furnace. And yet they have not done dreaming these their pleasant Dreams, but encourage others, as much as in them lies, to the same Happiness. And at last, when they are quite lost in all their Expectations, they chear up themselves with this Sentence, [1] ' In great things the very attempt is enough '; and then complain of the shortness of man's life, that is not sufficient for so great an Undertaking.

[1] In magnis vel voluisse sat est.

And then for Gamesters, I am a little doubtful whether they are to be admitted into our Colledge ; and yet 'tis a foolish and ridiculous sight to see some addicted so to 't, that they can no sooner hear the ratling of the Dice but their heart leaps and dances again. And then when time after time they are so far drawn on with the hopes of winning that they have made shipwrack of all, and having split their Ship on that Rock of Dice, [1] no less terrible than the Bishop and 's Clerks, scarce got alive to shore, they chuse rather to cheat any man of their just Debts than not pay the money they lost, lest otherwise, forsooth, they be thought no men of their words. Again what is it, I pray, to see old fellows and half blind to play with Spectacles ? Nay and when a justly-deserv'd Gout has knotted their Knuckles, to hire a Caster, or one that may put the Dice in the Box for them ? A pleasant thing, I must confess, did it not for the most gart end in quarrels, and therefore belongs rather to the Furies than Me.

But there is no doubt but that that kind of men are wholly ours, who love to hear or tell

[1] non paulo formidabiliorem Malea.

feign'd Miracles and strange lyes, and are never
weary of any Tale, though never so long, so it
be of Ghosts, Spirits, Goblings, Devils, or the
like; which the farther they are from truth,
the more readily they are believ'd and the more
do they tickle their itching ears. And these
serve not only to pass away time, but bring
profit, especially to Masse Priests and Pardoners.
And next to these are they that have gotten
a foolish but pleasant perswasion, that if they
can but see a Wodden or painted Polypheme
Christopher, they shall not die that day; or
do but salute a carv'd-Barbara, in the usual
set Form, that he shall return safe from Battail;
or make his application to Erasmus on certain
days with some small Wax Candles and proper
Prayers, that he shall quickly be rich. Nay,
they have gotten an Hercules, another Hippo-
lytus, and a St. George, whose Horse most
religiously set out with Trappings and Bosses
there wants little but they worship; however,
they endeavour to make him their friend by
some Present or other; and to swear by his
Master's Brazen Helmet is an Oath for a Prince.
Or what should I say of them that hugg them-

selves with their counterfeit Pardons; that
have measur'd Purgatory by an Hour-glass, and
can without the least mistake demonstrate its
Ages, Years, Moneths, Days, Hours, Minutes,
and Seconds, as it were in a Mathematical
Table ? Or what of those who, having confidence
in certain Magical charms and short Prayers
invented by some pious Impostour, either for
his Soul's health or profit's sake, promise to
themselves every thing : Wealth, Honour,
Pleasure, Plenty, good Health, long Life, lively
Old-age, and the next place to Christ in the
other World, which yet they desire may not
happen too soon, that is to say before the
pleasures of this life have left them ?

And now suppose some Merchant, Souldier,
or Judge, out of so many Rapines, parts with
some small piece of money. He straight conceives all that sink of his whole life quite cleans'd ;
so many Perjuries, so many Lusts, so many
Debaucheries, so many Contentions, so many
Murders, so many Deceipts, so many breaches
of Trust, so many Treacheries bought off, as
it were by compact; and so bought off that
they may begin upon a new score. But what is

more foolish than those, or rather more happy, who daily reciting those seven verses of the Psalms promise to themselves more than the top of Felicity? which Magical verses some Devil or other, a merry one without doubt but more a Blab of his Tongue than crafty, is believ'd to have discover'd to St. Bernard, but not without a Trick. And these are so foolish that I am half asham'd of 'em my self, and yet they are approv'd, and that not onely by the common people, but even the Professors of Religion. And what, are not they also almost the same where several Countryes avouch to themselves their peculiar Saint, and as every one of them has his particular gift, so also his particular Form of Worship? As, one is good for the Tooth-ach; another, for Groaning-women; a third, for Stollen Goods; a fourth, for making a Voyage Prosperous; and a fifth, to cure Sheep of the Rot; and so of the rest, for it would be too tedious to run over all. And some there are that are good for more things than one; but chiefly, the Virgin Mother, to whom the common people do in a manner attribute more than to the Son.

Yet what do they beg of these Saints but what belongs to Folly? To examine it a little. Among all those offerings which are so frequently hung up in Churches, nay up to the very Roof of some of 'em, did you ever see the least acknowledgment from any one that had left his Folly, or grown a Hair's-breadth the wiser? One scapes a Shipwrack, and gets safe to Shore. Another, run through in a Duel, recovers. Another, while the rest were fighting, ran out of the Field, no less luckily than valiantly. Another, condemn'd to be hang'd, by the favour of some Saint or other, a friend to Thieves, got off himself by impeaching his fellows. Another escap'd by breaking Prison. Another recover'd from his Feaver in spight of his Physitian. Another's poison turning to a loosness prov'd his Remedy rather than Death; and that to his Wife's no small sorrow, in that she lost both her labour and her charge. Another's Cart broke, and he sav'd his Horses. Another preserv'd from the fall of a House. All these hang up their Tablets, but no one gives thanks for his recovery from Folly; so sweet a thing it is not to be Wise, that on the contrary men rather pray against any thing than Folly.

But why do I lanch out into this Ocean of Superstitions? [1]Had I an hundred Tongues, as many Mouthes, and a Voice never so strong, yet were I not able to run over the several sorts of Fools, or all the names of Folly; so thick do they swarm every where. And yet our Priests make no scruple to receive and cherish 'em, as proper instruments of profit; whereas if some scurvy Wise fellow should step up, and speak things as they are, as, To live well is the way to dye well; The best way to get quit of sin is to add to the money thou giv'st, the Hatred of sin, Tears, Watchings, Prayers, Fastings, and amendment of life; Such or such a Saint will favour thee, if thou imitatest his life;—these, I say, and the like, should this Wise man chat to the people, from what happiness into how great troubles would he draw 'em?

Of this Colledge also are they who in their lifetime appoint with what solemnity they'll be buried, and particularly set down how many Torches, how many Mourners, how many

[1] Non mihi si centum linguae sint, oraque centum,
Ferrea vox, omnes fatuorum evolvere formas,
Omnia stultitiae percurrere nomina possim:

Singers, how many Alms-men they will have at it ; as if any sense of it could come to them, or that it were a shame to them that their Corpse were not honourably interr'd ; so curious are they herein, as if, like the Ædiles of old, these were to present some Shews or Banquet to the people.

And though I am in hast, yet I cannot yet pass by them who, though they differ nothing from the meanest Cobler, yet 'tis scarcely credible how they flatter themselves with the empty Title of Nobility. One derives his Pedigree from Æneas, another from Brutus, a third from [1] the Star by the Tail of Ursa Major. They shew you on every side the Statues and Pictures of their Ancestours ; run over their great Grandfathers and great great Grandfathers of both Lines, and the Antient Matches of their Families ; when themselves yet are but once remov'd from a Statue, if not worse than those trifles they boast of. And yet by means of this pleasant self-love they live a happy life. Nor are they less Fools who admire these Beasts as if they were Gods.

But what do I speak of any one or 'tother

[1] ad Arcturum.

particular kind of men, as if this self-Love had not the same effect every where, and render'd most men superabundantly happy? As when a fellow, more deform'd than a Baboon, shall believe himself handsomer than Homer's Nireus. Another, as soon as he can draw two or three lines with a Compass, presently think himself an Euclid. A third, [1] that understands Musick no more than my Horse, and for his voice [2] as hoarse as a Dunghil-Cock, shall yet conceive himself another Hermogenes. But of all madness that's the most pleasant, when a man, seeing another any way excellent in what he pretends to himself, makes his boasts of it as confidently as if it were his own. And such was that rich fellow in Seneca, who when ever he told a story had his servants at his elbow tò prompt him the names; and to that height had they flatter'd him, that he did not question but he might venture a rubber at cuffs, a man otherwise so weak he could scarce stand, onely presuming on this, that he had a company of sturdy servants about him.

[1] Ὄνος πρὸς λύραν.

[2] Quo deterius nec Ille sonat, quo mordetur gallina marito.

Or to what purpose is it I should mind ye
of our professors of Arts? Forasmuch as this
Self-love is so natural to them all, that they
had rather part with their Father's land than
their foolish Opinions; but chiefly Players,
Fidlers, Orators, and Poets, of which the more
ignorant each of them is, the more insolently
he pleases himself, that is to say Vaunts and
Spreads out his Plumes. And [1] like lips find
like Lettice; nay, the more foolish any thing
is, the more 'tis admir'd; the greater number
being ever tickled at the worst things, because,
as I said before, most men are so subject to Folly.
And therefore if the more foolish a man is, the
more he pleases himself and is admir'd by others,
to what purpose should he beat his brains about
true knowledg, which first will cost him dear,
and next render him the more troublesome and
less confident, and, lastly, please onely a few?

And now I consider it, Nature has planted, not
onely in particular men but even in every Nation,
and scarce any City is there without it, a kind
of common self-love. And hence is it that
the English, besides other things, particularly

[1] Inveniunt similes labra lactucas.

challenge to themselves Beauty, Musick, and Feasting. The Scots are proud of their Nobility, Alliance to the Crown, and Logical Subtilties. The French think themselves the onely well-bred men. The Parisians, excluding all others, arrogate to themselves the onely knowledg of Divinity. The Italians affirm they are the onely Masters of good Letters and Eloquence, and flatter themselves on this account, that of all others they onely are not barbarous. In which kind of happiness those of Rome claim the first place, still dreaming to themselves of somewhat, I know not what, of old Rome. The Venetians fancy themselves happy in the opinion of their Nobility. The Greeks, as if they were the onely Authors of Sciences, swell themselves with the Titles of the Ancient Heroes. The Turk, and all that sink of the truly barbarous, challenge to themselves the onely glory of Religion, and laugh at Christians as superstitious. And much more pleasantly the Jews expect to this day the coming of the Messias, and so obstinately contend for their Law of Moses. The Spaniards give place to none in the reputation of Souldiery. The Germans pride themselves in their Talness of Stature and skill in Magick.

And, not to instance in every particular, you see, I conceive, how much satisfaction this Self-love, who has a Sister also not unlike her self call'd Flattery, begets every where; for Self-love is no more than the soothing of a man's self, which, done to another, is flattery. And though perhaps at this day it may be thought infamous, yet it is so only with them that are more taken with words than things. They think truth is inconsistent with flattery; but that it is much otherwise we may learn from the examples of brute Beasts. What more fawning than a Dog? and yet what more trusty? What has more of those little tricks than a Squirrel? and yet what more loving to man? Unless, perhaps you'll say, Men had better converse with fierce Lions, merciless Tigers, and furious Leopards. For that flattery is the most perni-cious of all things, by means of which some treacherous persons and mockers have run the credulous into such mischief. But this of mine proceeds from a certain gentleness and upright-ness of mind, and comes nearer to Vertue than

its opposite, Austerity, or a Morose and troublesome peevishness, as Horace calls it. This
supports the dejected, relieves the distressed,
encourages the fainting, awakens the stupid,
refreshes the sick, supples the untractable, joyns
loves together, and keeps them so joyn'd. It
entices children to take their learning, makes
old men frolick, and, under the colour of praise,
does without offence both tell Princes their
faults and shew them the way to amend 'em.
In short, it makes every man the more jocund
and acceptable to himself, which is the chiefest
point of felicity. Agen, what is more friendly
than when [1] two horses scrub one another?
And to say nothing of it, that it's a main part
of that fam'd eloquence, the better part of
Physick, and the onely thing in Poetry; 'tis
the delight and relish of all humane Society.

But 'tis a sad thing, they say, to be mistaken.
Nay rather, he is most miserable that is not so.
For they are quite beside the mark that place
the Happiness of men in Things themselves,
since it onely depends upon Opinion. For so
great is the obscurity and variety of humane

[1] Mutuum muli scabunt.

affairs, that nothing can be clearly known, as it is truly said by our Academicks, the least insolent of all the Philosophers; or if it could, it would but obstruct the pleasure of life. Lastly, the mind of man is so fram'd that it is rather taken with false colours than truth; of which if any one has a mind to make the experiment, let him go to Church and hear Sermons, in which if there be any thing serious deliver'd, the Auditory is either asleep, yawning, or weary of 't; but if the Preacher—pardon my mistake, I would have said Declaimer—, as too often it happens, fall but into an old Wife's story, they 're presently awake, prick up their ears and gape after it. In like manner, if there be any Poetical Saint, or one of whom there goes more stories than ordinary, as for example, a George, a Christopher, or a Barbara, you shall see him more religiously worshipp'd than Peter, Paul, or even Christ himself. But these things are not for this place.

And now at how cheap a rate is this happiness purchast! Forasmuch as to the thing it self a man's whole endeavour is requir'd, be it never so inconsiderable; but the opinion of it is easily taken up, which yet conduceth as much or more to happiness. For suppose a man were eating rotten Stockfish, the very smell of which would choak another, and yet believ'd it a dish for the Gods, what difference is there as to his happiness? Whereas on the contrary, if another's stomack should turn at a Sturgion, wherein, I pray, is he happier than t' other? If a man have a crooked, ill-favour'd Wife, who yet in his Eye may stand in competition with Venus, is it not the same as if she were truly beautiful? Or if seeing an ugly, ill-painted piece, he should admire the work as believing it some great Master's hand, were he not much happier, think ye, than they that buy such things at vast rates, and yet perhaps reap less pleasure from 'em than t' other? I know one of my name that gave his new marri'd Wife some counterfeit Jewels, and, as he was a pleasant Droll, perswaded her that they were not onely right, but of an inestimable price; and what difference, I pray, to her, that was as well pleas'd and contented with Glass, and kept it as warily as if 't 'ad been a treasure? In the mean time the Husband sav'd his money, and had this advantage

of her folly, that he oblig'd her as much as if
he had bought 'em at a great rate. Or what
difference, think ye, between those in Plato's
imaginary Cave, that stand gaping at the
Shadows and Figures of things, so they please
themselves and have no need to wish ; and that
Wise Man, who, being got loose from 'em, sees
things truly as they are ? Whereas that Cobler
in Lucian, if he might always have continu'd
his Golden Dreams, he would never have desir'd
any other happiness. So then there is no
difference ; or, if there be, the Fools ha' the
'vantage : first, in that their happiness costs
them least, that is to say, onely some small
perswasion; next, that they enjoy it in common.
And the possession of no good can be delightful
without a companion. For who does not know
what a dearth there is of Wise men, if yet any one
be to be found ? and though the Greeks for these
so many ages have accounted upon seaven only,
yet so help me Hercules, do but examine 'em
narrowly, and I'll be hang'd if ye find one half-
witted fellow, nay or so. much as one quarter
of a Wise man, amongst 'em all.

For whereas among the many praises of

Bacchus they reckon this the chief, that he washeth away cares, and that too in an instant; do but sleep off his weak spirits, and they come on agen, [1] as we say, on horseback. But how much larger and more present is the benefit ye receive by me, since, as it were with a perpetual drunkenness, I fill your minds with Mirth, Fancies and Jollities, and that too without any trouble? Nor is there any man living whom I let be without it; whereas the gifts of the Gods are scambled, some to one and some to another. The sprightly delicious Wine that drives away cares and leaves such a Flavour behind it, grows not every where. Beauty, the gift of Venus, happens to few; and to fewer gives Mercury Eloquence. Hercules makes not every one rich. Homer's Jupiter bestows not Empire on all men. Mars oftentimes favours neither side. Many return sad from Apollo's Oracle. Phoebus sometimes shoots a Plague amongst us. Neptune drowns more than he saves: to say nothing of those [2] mischievous Gods, Plutoes, Ates, Punishments, Feavours and the like, not Gods but Executioners. I

[1] albis, ut aiunt, quadrigis.　　　[2] Vaejoves.

am that only Folly that so readily and indifferently bestow my benefits on all. Nor do I look to be entreated, or am I subject to take pett, and require an expiatory sacrifice if some Ceremony be omitted. Nor do I [1] beat heaven and earth together, if, when the rest of the Gods are invited, I am past by or not admitted to the steam of their Sacrifices. For the rest of the Gods are so curious in this point, that such an omission may chance to spoil a man's business; and therefore one had as good ev'n let 'em alone as worship 'em: just like some men, who are so hard to please, and withall so ready to do mischief, that 'tis better be a stranger than have any familiarity with 'em.

But no man, you'll say, ever sacrific'd to Folly, or built me a Temple. And troth, as I said before, I cannot but wonder at the ingratitude; yet because I am easie to be entreated, I take this also in good part, though truelie I can scarce request it. For why should I require Incense, Wafers, a Goat or Sow, when all men pay me that worship every where, which is so much approv'd even by our very Divines? Unless perhaps

[1] coelum terris et mare coelo.

I should envy Diana, that her Sacrifices are mingled with Humane blood. Then do I conceive my self most religiouslie worshipp'd, when every where, as 'tis generally done, men embrace me in their Minds, express me in their Manners, and represent me in their Lives ; which worship of the Saints is not so ordinary among Christians. How many are there that burn Candles to the Virgin Mother, and that too at noon day, when there 's no need of 'em ! But how few are there that studie to imitate her in pureness of Life, Humility and love of Heavenlie things, which is the true worship and most acceptable to Heaven ! Besides why should I desire a Temple, when the whole world is my Temple, and I'm deceiv'd or 'tis a goodly one? Nor can I want Priests, but in a Land where there are no men. Nor am I yet so foolish as to require Statues or painted Images, which do often obstruct my Worship, since among the stupid and gross multitude those Figures are worshipt for the Saints themselves. And so it would fare with me, as it doth with them that are turn'd out of doors by their Substitutes. No, I have Statues enough, and as many as there are Men ;

every one bearing my lively Resemblance in
his Face, how unwilling so ever he be to the
contrary. And therefore there is no reason why
I should envie the rest of the Gods, if in particular places they have their particular worship,
and that too on set-days—as Phoebus at
Rhodes; at Cyprus, Venus; at Argos, Juno;
at Athens, Minerva; in Olympus, Jupiter; at
Tarentum, Neptune; and near the Hellespont,
Priapus—; as long as the World in general
performs me every day much better Sacrifices.

Wherein notwithstanding if I shall seem to
any one to have spoken more boldlie than trulie,
let us, if ye please, look a little into the lives of
men, and it will easily appear not onely how
much they owe to me, but how much they
esteem me even from the highest to the lowest.
And yet we will not run over the lives of everie
one, for that would be too long; but onelie
some few of the great ones, from whence we
shall easilie conjecture the rest. For to what
purpose is it to say any thing of the common
people, who without dispute are whollie mine?
For they abound every where with so many
several sorts of Folly, and are everie day so busie

in inventing new, that a thousand Democriti
are too few for so general a laughter, though
there were another Democritus to laugh at them
too. 'Tis almost incredible what Sport and
Pastime they dailie make the Gods ; for though
they set aside their sober forenoon hours to
dispatch business and receive prayers, yet when
they begin to be well whitled with Nectar, and
cannot think of anything that's serious, they
get 'em up into some part of Heaven that has
better prospect than other, and thence look
down upon the actions of men. Nor is there
anie thing that pleases 'em better. Good,
good ! what an excellent sight 'tis ! How many
several Hurlie-burlies of Fools ! for I my self
sometimes sit among those Poetical Gods.

Here's one desperatelie in love with a young
Wench, and the more she sleights him the more
outragiouslie he loves her. Another marries
a woman's money, not her self. Another's
jealousie keeps more eyes on her than Argos.
Another becomes a Mourner, and how foolishlie
he carries it ! nay, hires others to bear him
companie, to make it more ridiculous. Another
weeps over his Mother in Law's Grave. Another

spends all he can rap and run on his Bellie, to
be the more hungry after it. Another thinks
there is no happiness but in sleep and idleness.
Another turmoils himself about other men's
business, and neglects his own. Another thinks
himself rich in taking up moneys and changing
Securities, as we say borrowing of Peter to pay
Paul, and in a short time becomes bankrupt.
Another starves himself to enrich his Heir.
Another for a small and incertain gain exposes
his life to the casualties of Seas and Winds,
which yet no money can restore. Another had
rather get Riches by War than live peaceably at
home. And some there are that think them
easiest attain'd by courting old childless men
with Presents ; and others again by making
rich old women believe they love 'm ; both
which afford the Gods most excellent pastime,
to see them cheated by those persons they
thought to have over-cach't. But the most
foolish and basest of all others are our Merchants,
to wit such as venture on every thing be it never
so dishonest, and manage it no better ; who
though they lie by no allowance, swear and for-
swear, steal, cozen, and cheat, yet shufle them-

selves into the first rank, and all because they have Gold Rings on their Fingers. Nor are they without their flattering Friers that admire them and give 'em openly the title of Honourable, in hopes, no doubt, to get some small snip of 't themselves.

There are also a kind of Pythagoreans, with whom all things are so common, that if they get any thing under their Cloaks, they make no more scruple of carrying it away than if 'twere their own by inheritance. There are others too that are onely rich in conceit, and while they fancie to themselves pleasant dreams, conceive that enough to make them happy. Some desire to be accounted wealthy abroad, and are yet ready to starve at home. One makes what haste he can to set all going, and another rakes it together by right or wrong. This man is ever labouring for publick honours; and another lies sleeping in a Chimney-corner. A great many undertake endless Suites, and outvie one another who shall most enrich the Delatory Judge or Corrupt Advocate. One is all for Innovations; and another for some great-he-knows-not-what. Another leaves his Wife and Children at home, and goes to Jerusalem, Rome, or in Pilgrimage

to St. James's, where he has no business. In
short, if a man like Menippus of old could look
down from the Moon, and behold those innumerable rufflings of Mankind, he would think
he saw a swarm of Flies and Gnats quarrelling
among themselves, fighting, laying Traps for
one another, snatching, playing, wantoning,
growing up, falling, and dying. Nor is it to be
believ'd what stir, what broils this little creature
raiseth, and yet in how short a time it comes to
nothing its self; while sometimes War, other-
times Pestilence, sweeps off many thousands of
'em together.

But let me be most foolish my self, and one
whom Democritus may not onely laugh at but
flout, if I go one foot further in the discovery
of the Follies and Madnesses of the common
people. I'll betake me to them that carry
the reputation of Wise men, and hunt after that
golden Bough, as says the Proverb. Amongst
whom the Grammarians hold the first place,
a generation of men than whom nothing would be
more miserable, nothing more perplext, nothing
more hated of the Gods, did not I allay the
troubles of that pittiful Profession with a certain

kind of pleasant madness. For they are not onely subject to those [1] five curses with which Homer begins his Iliads, as says the Greek Epigramme, but six hundred; as being ever hunger-starv'd, and slovens in their Schools —Schools, did I say? Nay, rather [2] Cloisters, Bridwells or Slaughter-houses—, grown old among a company of boyes, deaf with their noise, and pin'd away with stench and nastiness. And yet by my courtesie it is that they think themselves the most excellent of all men; so greatly do they please themselves in frighting a company of fearful boyes, with a thundring voice and big looks; tormenting them with Ferules, Rods, and Whips; and, laying about 'em without fear or wit, imitate the Ass in the Lion's skin. In the mean time all that nastiness seems absolute Spruceness, that Stench a Perfume, and that miserable slaverie a Kingdom, and such too as they would not change their Tyrannie for Phalaris' or Dionysius's Empire. Nor are they less happy in that new Opinion they have taken up of being learned; for whereas most of 'em beat into boys' heads nothing but foolish Toyes,

---

[1] πέντε κατάραις.   [2] φροντιστηρίοις.

yet, ye good Gods! what Palemon, what
Donatus, do they not scorn in comparison of
themselves? And so, I know not by what tricks,
they bring it about that to their boys' foolish
Mothers and dolt-headed Fathers they pass for
such as they fancy themselves. Add to this
that other pleasure of theirs, that if any of 'em
happen to find out who was Anchises's Mother,
or pick out of some worm-eaten Manuscript
a word not commonly known, as suppose it
Bubsequa for a Cowheard, Bovinator for a
Wrangler, Manticulator for a Cutpurse; or dig
up the ruines of some ancient Monument, with
the letters half eaten out; O Jupiter! what
towrings! what triumphs! what commenda-
tions! as if they had conquer'd Africa, or taken
in Babylon.

But what of this when they give up and down
their foolish insipid verses, and there wants not
others that admire 'em as much? They believe
presently that Virgil's soul is transmigrated into
them! But nothing like this, when with
mutual complements they praise, admire and
claw one another. Whereas if another do but
slip a word, and one more quick-sighted than

the rest discover it by accident, [1] O Hercules! what uproars, what bickerings, what taunts, what invectives! If I lye, let me have the ill will of all the Grammarians. I knew in my time [2] one of many Arts, a Grecian, a Latinist, a Mathematician, a Philosopher, a Physitian, [3] a Man master of 'em all, and sixty years of age, who, laying by all the rest, perplext and tormented himself for above twenty years in the study of Grammar; fully reckoning himself a Prince if he might but live so long till he could certainly determine how the Eight parts of Speech were to be distinguisht, which none of the Greeks or Latines had yet fully clear'd: as if it were a matter to be decided by the Sword, if a man made an Adverb of a Conjunction. And for this cause is it that we have as many Grammars as Grammarians; nay more, forasmuch as my friend Aldus has giv'n us above five, not passing by any kind of Grammar, how barbarously or tediously soever compil'd, which he has not turn'd over and examin'd; envying every man's attempts in this kind, how

---

[1] Ἡράκλεις.   [2] πολυτεχνύτατον quendam.

[3] κὰ ταῦτα βασιλικὸν.

foolish so ever, and desperately concern'd for fear another should forestal him of his glory, and the labours of so many years perish. And now, whether had you rather call this Madness or Folly? It is no great matter to me whether, so long as ye confess it is by my means that a creature, otherwise the most miserable of all others, is rais'd to that height of felicity that he has no desire to change his condition with the King of Persia.

The Poets, I must confess, are not altogether so much beholding to me, though 'tis agreed of all hands they are of my partie too; because they are a free kind of people, not restrain'd or limited to any thing, and all their studies aim at nothing more than to tickle the ears of fools with meer trifles and ridiculous fables. And yet they are so bold upon 't, that you'll scarce believe how they not onely assure themselves of immortality and a life like the Gods, but promise it to others too. And to this order, before all others, Self-love and Flattery are more peculiarly appendant; nor am I worshipt by any sort of men with more plainness or greater constancy.

And then, for the Rhetoricians, though they now and then shuffle and cut with the Philosopher, yet that these two are of my faction also, though many other Arguments might be produc'd, this clearly evinces it; that besides their other trifles, they have written so much and so exquisitely of Fooling. And so, who ever he were that writ of the Art of Rhetorick to Herennius, he reckons Folly as a species of wit. And Quintilian, the Soveraign of this Order, has a Chapter touching Laughter more prolixe than an Iliad. In fine, they attribute so much to Folly, that what many times cannot be clear'd with the best Arguments, is yet now and then put off with a jest: unless, perhaps you'll say, 'tis no part of Folly to provoke laughter, and that artificially.

Of the same batch also are they that hunt after immortality of Fame by setting out Books. Of whom, though all of 'em are endebted to me, yet in the first place are they that nothing but daub Paper with their empty Toyes. For they that write learnedly to the understanding of a few Scholers, and refuse not to stand the test of a Persius or Laelius, seem to me rather

to be pittied than happy, as persons that are
ever tormenting themselves ; Adding, Changing,
Putting in, Blotting out, Revising, Reprinting,
showing 't to friends, [1] and nine years in cor-
recting, yet never fully satisfied ; at so great a
rate do they purchase this vain reward, to wit,
Praise, and that too of a very few, with so many
watchings, so much sweat, so much vexation
and loss of sleep, the most pretious of all things.
Add to this the waste of health, spoil of com-
plexion, weakness of eyes or rather blindness,
poverty, envie, abstinence from pleasure, over-
hasty Old-age, untimely death, and the like ;
so highly does this Wise man value the approba-
tion of one or two blear-ey'd fellows. But how
much happier is this my Writer's dotage, who
never studies for any thing, but puts in writing
what ever he pleases or what comes first in his
head, though it be but his dreams ; and all this
with small waste of Paper, as well knowing that
the vainer those Trifles are, the higher esteem
they will have with the greater number, that is
to say all the fools and unlearned. And what
matter is it to sleight those few learned, if yet

[1] nonumque prematur in annum.

they ever read them? Or of what authority
will the censure of so few Wise men be against
so great a Cloud of Gainsayers?

But they are the wiser that put out other
men's works for their own, and transfer that
glory which others with great pains have
obtain'd to themselves; relying on this, that
they conceive, though it should so happen that
their theft be never so plainly detected, that yet
they should enjoy the pleasure of it for the
present. And 'tis worth one's while to consider
how they please themselves when they are
applauded by the common people, pointed at
in a Croud, [1] ' This is that excellent person ';
lie on Book-sellers' stalls; and in the top of every
Page have three hard words read, but chiefly
Exotick, and next degree to conjuring; which,
by the immortal Gods! what are they but meer
words? And agen, if ye consider the world,
by how few understood, and prais'd by fewer!
for even amongst the unlearned there are different palates. Or what is it that their own
very names are often conterfeit, or borrow'd
from some Books of the Antients? When one

[1] οὗτος ἐστὶν ὁ δεινὸς ἐκεῖνος.

stiles himself Telemachus, another Sthenelus,
a third Laertes, a fourth Polycrates, a fifth
Thrasymachus. So that there is no difference
whether they Title their Books with the 'Tale
of a Tub', or, according to the Philosophers,
by Alpha, Beta.

But the most pleasant of all is to see them
praise one another with Reciprocal Epistles,
Verses, and Encomiums ; Fools their fellow-
Fools, and Dunces their brother Dunces. This,
in t' other's opinion, is an absolute Alcaeus ;
and the other, in his, a very Callimachus. He
looks upon Tully as nothing to t' other, and
t' other again pronunces him more learned than
Plato. And sometimes too they pick out their
Antagonist, and think to raise themselves a
Fame by writing one against t' other ; while
[1] the giddy multitude are so long divided to
whether o' th' two they shall determine the
Victory, till each goes off Conquerour, and, as
if he had done some great Action, fancies
himself a Triumph. And now Wise Men laugh
at these things as foolish, as indeed they are.
Who denies it ? Yet in the mean time, such is

[1] Scinditur incertum studia in contraria vulgus.

my kindness to them, they live a merry life, and
would not change their imaginary Triumphs,
no, not with the Scipioes. While yet those
Learned men, though they laugh their fill and
reap the benefit of t'others' Folly, cannot without ingratitude denie but that even they too are
not a little beholding to me themselves.

And amongst them our Advocates challenge
the first place, nor is there anie sort of people
that please themselves like them : for while
they dailie roul Sisyphus his stone ; and quote
ye a thousand cases, as it were in a breath, no
matter how little to the purpose ; and heap
Glosses upon Glosses, and Opinions on the neck
of Opinions ; they bring it at last to this pass,
that that studie of all other seems the most
difficult. Add to these, our Logicians and
Sophisters, a generation of men [1]more pratling
than an Echo, and the worst of 'em able to out-
chat an hundred of the best pickt Gossips.
And yet their condition would be much better
were they onely full of words, and not so given
to scolding, that they most obstinatelie hack and
hew one another [2]about a matter of nothing,

[1] aere Dodonaeo loquacius.   [2] de lana caprina.

and make such a sputter about Terms and
Words, till they have quite lost the Sense. And
yet they are so happy in the good opinion of
themselves, that as soon as they are furnisht with
two or three Syllogisms, they dare boldly enter
the Lists against any Man upon any Point ;
as not doubting but to run him down with
noise, though the Opponent were another
Stentor.

And next these come our Philosophers, so
much reverenc'd for their Fur'd Gowns and
Starcht Beards, that they look upon themselves
as the onely Wise Men, and all others as
Shadows. And yet how pleasantly do they dote
while they frame in their heads innumerable
worlds ; measure out the Sun, the Moon, the
Stars, nay and Heaven it self, as it were with
a pair of Compasses ; lay down the Causes of
Lightning, Winds, Eclipses, and other the like
Inexplicable Matters ; and all this too without
the least doubting, as if they were Nature's
Secretaries, or dropt down among us from the
Council of the Gods ; while in the mean time
Nature laughs at them and all their blind
conjectures. For, that they know nothing, even

this is a sufficient Argument, that they do 'nt
agree amongst themselves, and are so indemon-
strable as to others touching every particular.
These, though they have not the least degree of
knowledge, profess yet that they have master'd
all ; nay, though they neither know themselves,
nor perceive a Ditch or Block that lies in their
way, for that perhaps most of them are half
blind, or their wits a wooll-gathering, yet give
out that they have discovr'd Ideas, Universali-
ties, separated Forms, first Matters, Quiddities,
Ecceities, Formalities, and the like stuff ; things
so thin and bodiless, that I believe even Lynceus
himself were not able to perceive 'em. But
then chiefly do they disdain [1] the unhallow'd
Croud, as often as with their Triangles, Quad-
rangles, Circles and the like Mathematical
Devices, more confounded than a Labyrinth,
and Letters dispos'd one against t' other, as
it were in Battle-Array, they cast a mist before
the eyes of the ignorant. Nor is there wanting
of this kind some that pretend to foretell things
by the Stars, and make promises of Miracles
beyond all things of Southsaying, and are so

[1] prophanum vulgus.

fortunate as to meet with people that believe
'em.

But perhaps I had better pass over our
Divines in silence [1] and not stir this Pool, or
touch this fair but unsavoury Plant; as a kind
of men that are supercilious beyond comparison, and to that too, implacable; lest
setting 'em about my ears, they attaque me by
Troops, and force me to a Recantation-Sermon,
which if I refuse, they streight pronounce me
an Heretick. For this is the Thunder-bolt with
which they fright those whom they are resolv'd
not to favour. And truly, though there are few
others that less willingly acknowledge the kind-
nesses I have done them, yet even these too
stand fast bound to me upon no ordinary
accounts; whil'st being happy in their own
Opinion, and as if they dwelt in the third
Heaven, they look with Haughtiness on all
others as poor creeping things, and could
almost find in their hearts to pitie 'em; whilst
hedg'd in with so many Magisterial Definitions,
Conclusions, Corollaries, Propositions Explicit
and Implicit, they abound with so many [2] start-

---

[1] καὶ ταύτην Καμαρίναν μὴ κινεῖν.   [2] κρησφυγέτοις.

ing-holes, that Vulcan's Net cannot hold 'em
so fast, but they'll slip through with their
distinctions ; with which they so easily cut all
knots asunder that a Hatchet could not have
done it better, so plentiful are they in their
new-found Words and prodigious Terms.
Besides, whil'st they explicate the most hidden
Mysteries according to their own fancie :—as,
how the World was first made ; how Original
Sin is deriv'd to Posterity ; in what manner,
how much room, and how long time, Christ
lay in the Virgin's Womb ; how Accidents
subsist in the Eucharist without their Subject.

But these are common and threadbare ; these
are worthy of our great and illuminated Divines,
as the world calls 'em ! At these, if ever they
fall a thwart 'em, they prick up :—as, whether
there was any instant of time in the generation
of the Second Person ; whether there be more
than one Filiation in Christ ; whether it be
a possible Proposition that God the Father
hates the Son ; or whether it was possible that
Christ could have taken upon Him the likeness
of a Woman, or of the Devil, or of an Ass, or
of a Stone, or of a Gourd ; and then how that

Gourd should have Preach't, wrought Miracles,
or been hung on the Cross; and, what Peter
had Consecrated, if he had administred the
Sacrament at what time the Body of Christ
hung upon the Cross; or whether at the same
time he might be said to be Man; whether
after the Resurrection there will be any eating
and drinking, since we are so much afraid of
hunger and thirst in this world. There are
infinite of these [1] subtile Trifles, and others
more subtile than these; of Notions, Relations,
Instants, Formalities, Quiddities, Ecceities,
which no one can perceive without a Lynceus
his eyes, that could look through a stone-wall,
and discover those things through the thickest
darkness that never were.

Add to this those their other Determinations,
and those too so contrary to common Opinion
that those Oracles of the Stoicks, which they call
Paradoxes, seem in comparison of these but
blockish and idle :—as, 'tis a lesser crime to kill
a thousand men than to set a stitch on a poor
man's shooe on the Sabbath-day; and that a
man should rather chuse that the whole world

[1] λεπτολεσχίαι.

with all Food and Raiment, as they say, should
perish, than tell a lye, though never so inconsiderable. And these most subtile subtilties
are rendred yet more subtile by the several
Methods of so many Schoolmen, that one might
sooner wind himself out of a Labyrinth than
the entanglements of the Realists, Nominalists,
Thomists, Albertists, Occamists, Scotists. Nor
have I nam'd all the several Sects, but onely
some of the chief; in all which there is so much
Doctrine and so much difficultie, that I may
well conceive the Apostles, had they been to
deal with these new kind of Divines, had needed
to have pray'd in aid of some other Spirit.

Paul knew what Faith was, and yet when he
saith, ' Faith is the Substance of things hop'd
for, and the Evidence of things not seen ', he
did not define it Doctor-like. And as he understood Charity well himself, so he did as Illogi-
cally divide and define it to others in his first
Epistle to the Corinthians, Chapter the thir-
teenth. And devoutly, no doubt, did the
Apostles consecrate the Eucharist; yet, had they
been askt the question touching the ' Terminus
a quo ' and the ' Terminus ad quem ' of Transub-

stantiation; of the manner how the same body
can be in several places at one and the same
time; of the difference the body of Christ has
in Heaven from that of the Cross, or this in the
Sacrament; in what punct of time Transub-
stantiation is, whereas Prayer, by means of which
it is, as being a discrete quantity, is transient;
they would not, I conceive, have answer'd with
the same subtilty as the Scotists Dispute and
Define it. They knew the Mother of Jesus; but
which of them has so Philosophically demon-
strated how she was preserv'd from Original
sin, as have done our Divines? Peter receiv'd
the Keyes, and from Him too that would not
have trusted them with a person unworthy;
yet whether he had understanding or no, I know
not, for certainly he never attain'd to that
subtilty to determine how he could have the
Key of knowledge that had no knowledge
himself. They Baptized far and near, and yet
taught no where what was the Formal, Material,
Efficient, and final cause of Baptisme; nor
made the least mention of delible and indelible
Characters. They worshipt, 'tis true, but in
Spirit, following herein no other than that of

the Gospel, 'God is a Spirit, and they that worship, must worship him in Spirit and Truth'; yet it does not appear it was at that time reveal'd to them that an Image sketcht on the Wall with a Cole, was to be worshipt with the same worship as Christ Himself, if at least the two 'fore fingers be stretcht out, the hair long and uncut, and have three Rayes about the Crown of the Head. For who can conceive these things, unless he has spent at least six and thirty years in the Philosophical and Supercoelestial Whims of Aristotle and the Schoolmen?

In like manner, the Apostles press to us Grace; but which of them distinguisheth between [1] free grace and grace that makes a man acceptable? They exhort us to good works, and yet determine not [2] what is the work working, and what a resting in the work done. They incite us to Charity, and yet make no difference between [3] Charity infus'd and Charity wrought in us by our own endeavours. Nor do they declare whether it be an Accident or a Sub-

[1] gratiam gratis datam et gratiam gratificantem.
[2] opus operans et opus operatum.
[3] infusam et acquisitam.

stance, a thing Created or Uncreated. They
detest and abominate sin, but let me not live
if they could define according to Art what that
is which we call Sin, unless perhaps they were
inspir'd by the spirit of the Scotists. Nor can
I be brought to believe that Paul, by whose
learning you may judge the rest, would have so
often condemn'd Questions, Disputes, Genea-
logies, and, as himself calls 'em, [1] 'Strifes of
words', if he had throughly understood those
subtilties ; especially when all the Debates and
Controversies of those times were rude and
blockish, in comparison of the more than
Chrysippean subtilties of our Masters. Although
yet the Gentlemen are so modest, that if they
meet with any thing written by the Apostles
not so smooth and even as might be expected
from a Master, they do not presently condemn
it, but handsomly bend it to their own purpose;
so great Respect and Honour do they give,
partly to Antiquity and partly to the name of
Apostle. And truly 'twere a kind of injustice
to require so great things of them that never
heard the least word from their Masters concern-

[1] λογομαχίας.

ing it. And so if the like happen in Chrysostome, Basil, Jerome, they think it enough to say, They are not oblig'd by 't.

The Apostles also confuted the Heathen Philosophers and Jews, a people than whom none more obstinate; but rather by their good Lives and Miracles than Syllogisms: and yet there was scarce one amongst 'em that was capable of understanding the least ' Quodlibet ' of the Scotists. But now, where is that Heathen or Heretick that must not presently stoop to such Wire-drawn subtilties, unless he be so thick-skul'd that he can't apprehend 'em, or so impudent as to hiss 'em down, or, being furnisht with the same Tricks, be able to make his party good with 'em? As if a man should set a Conjurer on work against a Conjurer, or fight with one hallowed Sword against another, which would prove no other than [1] a work to no purpose. For my own part I conceive the Christians would do much better, if instead of those dull Troops and Companies of Souldiers, with which they have manag'd their War with such doubtful success, they would send the

[1] Penelopes tela.

bauling Scotists, the most obstinate Occamists, and invincible Albertists to war against the Turks and Saracens; and they would see, I guess, a most pleasant Combate, and such a Victory as was never before. For who is so faint whom their devices will not enliven? who so stupid whom such spurrs can't quicken? or who so quick-sighted, before whose eyes they can't cast a mist?

But you'l say, I jest. Nor are ye without cause, since even amongst Divines themselves there are some that have learnt better, and are ready to turn their stomacks at those foolish subtilties of t' others. There are some that detest 'em as a kind of Sacriledge, and count it the height of Impiety to speak so irreverently of such hidden things, rather to be ador'd than explicated; to dispute of 'em with such profane and Heathenish niceties; to define 'em so arrogantly, and pollute the majestie of Divinity with such pithless and sordid terms and opinions. Mean time the others please, nay hug themselves in their happiness, and are so taken up with these pleasant trifles, that they have not so much leisure as to cast the least eye on the

Gospel or S. Paul's Epistles. And while they play the fool at this rate in their Schools, they make account the Universal Church would otherwise perish, unless, as the Poets fancy'd of Atlas that he supported Heaven with his shoulders, they underpropt t' other with their Syllogistical Buttresses. And how great a happiness is this, think ye? while, as if holy Writ were a Nose of Wax, they fashion and refashion it according to their pleasure; while they require that their own Conclusions, subscrib'd by two or three Schoolmen, be accounted greater than Solon's Laws, and prefer'd before the Papal Decretals; while, as Censors of the world, they force every one to a Recantation, that differs but a hair's bredth from the least of their Explicit or Implicit Determinations. And those too they pronounce like Oracles. This Proposition is scandalous; this Irreverent; this has a smatch of Heresie; this no very good sound : so that neither Baptisme, nor the Gospel, nor Paul, nor Peter, nor St. Jerome, nor St. Augustine, no nor [1] most Aristotelitotical Thomas himself, can make a man

---

[1] Ἀριστοτελικώτατος ipse Thomas.

a Christian, without these Batchelours too be
pleas'd to give him his grace. And the like
is their subtilty in judging; for who would
think he were no Christian that should say these
two Speeches 'Matula Putes' and 'matula Putet',
or 'Ollae fervere ' and ' ollam fervere' were not
both good Latine, unless their wisdomes had
taught us the contrary? who had deliver'd the
Church from such Mists of Errour, which yet no
one e're met with, had they not come out with
some University Seal for 't? And are they not
most happy while they do these things?

Then for what concerns Hell, how exactly
they describe every thing, as if they had been
conversant in that Common-wealth most part
of their time! Again, how do they frame in
their fancy new Orbes, adding to those we have
already an eighth! a goodly one, no doubt, and
spatious enough, lest perhaps their happy Souls
might lack room to walk in, entertain their
friends, and now and then play at Foot-ball.
And with these and a thousand the like fopperies
their heads are so full stufft and stretcht, that
I believe Jupiter's brain was not near so bigg
when, being in labour with Pallas, he was

beholding to the Midwifery of Vulcan's Axe. And therefore ye must not wonder if in their publique Disputes they are so bound about the head, lest otherwise perhaps their brains might leap out. Nay, I have sometimes laught my self, to see 'em so towre in their own opinion when they speak most barbarously; and when they Humh and Hawh so pitifully that none but one of their own Tribe can understand 'em, they call it heights which the Vulgar can't reach; for they say 'tis beneath the dignity of Divine Mysteries to be crampt and ty'd up to the narrow Rules of Grammarians: from whence we may conjecture the great Prerogative of Divines, if they onely have the priviledge of speaking corruptly, in which yet every Cobler thinks himself concern'd for his share. Lastly, they look upon themselves as somewhat more than Men, as often as they are devoutly saluted by the name of 'Our Masters', in which they fancy there lyes as much as in the Jews' [1] 'Jehovah'; and therefore they reckon it a crime if 'Magister noster' be written other than in Capital Letters; and if any one should preposterously say 'Noster

[1] τετραγράμματον.

magister ', he has at once overturn'd the whole
body of Divinity.

And next these come those that commonly
call themselves the Religious and Monks; most
false in both Titles, when both a great part
of 'em are farthest from Religion, and no men
swarm thicker in all places than themselves.
Nor can I think of any thing that could be more
miserable, did not I support 'em so many several
wayes. For whereas all men detest 'em to that
height, that they take it for ill luck to meet
one of 'em by chance, yet such is their happiness
that they flatter themselves. For first, they
reckon it one of the main Points of Piety if they
are so illiterate that they can't so much as read.
And then when they run over their Offices,
which they carry about 'em, rather by tale than
understanding, they believe the Gods more than
ordinarily pleas'd with their braying. And some
there are among 'em that put off their trumperies
at vast rates, yet roave up and down for the
bread they eat; nay, there is scarce an Inne,
Waggon, or Ship into which they intrude not,
to the no small damage of the Common-wealth
of Beggars. And yet, like pleasant fellows, with

all this Vileness, Ignorance, Rudeness and Impudence, they represent to us, for so they call it, the lives of the Apostles. Yet what is more pleasant than that they do all things by Rule and, as it were, a kind of Mathematicks, the least swerving from which were a crime beyond forgiveness :—as, how many knots their shooes must be ti'd with, of what colour every thing is, what distinction of habits, of what stuffe made, how many straws broad their Girdles and of what fashion, how many bushels wide their Cowle, how many fingers long their Hair, and how many hours sleep ; which exact equality, how disproportionable it is, among such variety of bodies and tempers, who is there that does not perceive it ? And yet by reason of these fooleries they not onely set slight by others, but each different Order, men otherwise professing Apostolical Charity, despise one another, and for the different wearing of a habit, or that 'tis of darker colour, they put all things in combustion. And amongst these there are some so rigidly Religious that their upper Garment is hair-Cloth, their inner of the finest Linnen ; and, on the contrary, others wear

Linnen without, and hair next their skins.
Others, agen, are as affraid to touch mony as
poyson, and yet neither forbear Wine nor
dallying with Women. In a word, 'tis their
onely care that none of 'em come near one
another in their manner of living, nor do they
endeavour how they may be like Christ, but
how they may differ among themselves.

And another great happiness they conceive in
their Names, while they call themselves Cor-
diliers, and among these too, some are Colletes,
some Minors, some Minims, some Crossed;
and agen, these are Benedictines, those Bernar-
dines; these Carmelites, those Augustines;
these Williamites, and those Jacobines; as if
it were not worth the while to be call'd Christians. And of these, a great part build so much
on their Ceremonies and petty Traditions of
Men, that they think one Heaven is too poor
a reward for so great merit; little dreaming
that the time will come when Christ, not regard-
ing any of these trifles, will call 'em to account
for His precept of Charity. One shall shew ye
a large Trough full of all kinds of Fish; another
tumble ye out so many bushels of Prayers;

another reckon ye so many myriads of Fasts, and
fetch 'em up agen in one dinner by eating till
he cracks agen; another produces more bundles
of Ceremonies than seven of the stoutest Ships
would be able to carry; another brags he has
not toucht a penny these three score Years
without two pair of Gloves at least upon his
hands; another wears a Cowl so lin'd with
grease that the poorest Tarpaulin would not
stoop to take it up; another will tell ye he has
liv'd these fifty five Years like a Spunge, con-
tinually fastned to the same place; another is
grown hoarse with his daily chanting; another
has contracted a Lethargy by his solitary living;
and another the Palsie in his Tongue for want
of speaking. But Christ, interrupting them in
their vanities, which otherwise were endless,
will ask 'em, 'Whence this new kind of Jews?
I acknowledge one Commandment, which is
truly mine, of which alone I hear nothing.
I promist, 'tis true, my Father's heritage, and
that without Parables, not to Cowls, odd
Prayers, and Fastings, but to the duties of Faith
and Charity. Nor can I acknowledge them that
least acknowledg their faults. They that would

seem holier than my self, let 'em if they list
possess to [1] themselves those three hundred
sixty five Heavens of Basilides the Heretick's
invention, or command them whose foolish
Traditions they have prefer'd before my Pre-
ceps, to erect them a new one'. When they shall
hear these things, and see common ordinary
persons preferr'd before 'em, with what countenance, think ye, will they behold one another?
In the mean time they are happy in their
hopes, and for this also they are beholding
to me.

And yet these kind of people, though they are
as it were of another Common-wealth, no man
dares despise ; especially those begging Friars,
because they are privie to all men's secrets by
means of Confessions, as they call 'em. Which
yet were no less than treason to discover, unless,
being got drunk, they have a mind to be pleasant,
and then all comes out, that is to say by hints
and conjectures, but suppressing the names.
But if any one should anger these Wasps, they'll
sufficiently revenge themselves in their publique
Sermons, and so point out their enemy by

[1] Abraxasiorum coelos.

circumlocutions that there's no one but understands whom 'tis they mean, unless he understand nothing at all ; nor will they give over
their barking [1] till you throw the Dogs a bone.
And now tell me, what Jugler or Mountebank
you had rather behold than hear them rhetori-
cally play the fool in their Preachments, and yet
most sweetly imitating what Rhetoricians have
written touching the Art of good speaking ?
Good God ! what several postures they have !
How they shift their voice, sing out their words,
skip up and down, and are ever and anon making
such new faces, that they confound all things
with noise ! and yet this Knack of theirs is no
less than a Mystery that runs in succession from
one brother to another ; which though it be
not lawful for me to know, however I'll venture
at it by conjectures.   And first they invoke
what ever they have scrapt from the Poets ;
and in the next place, if they are to discourse
of Charity, they take their rise from the river
Nilus ; or to set out the Mystery of the Cross,
from Bell and the Dragon ; or to dispute of
Fasting, from the twelve signs of the Zodiack ;

[1] quam in os offam objeceris.

or, being to preach of Faith, ground their matter on the square of a Circle.

I have heard my self one, and he no small fool, —I was mistaken, I would have said Scholar,— that being in a Famous Assembly explaining the Mystery of the Trinity, that he might both let 'em see his Learning was not ordinary, and withal satisfie some Theological ears, he took a new way, to wit from the Letters, Syllables, and the Word it self ; then from the Cohærence of the Nominative Case and the Verb, and the Adjective and Substantive : and while most of the Auditory wonder'd, and some of 'em mutter'd that of Horace, [1] ' what does all this Trumpery drive at ? ' at last he brought the matter to this head, that he would demonstrate that the Mystery of the Trinity was so clearly exprest in the very Rudiments of Grammar, that the best Mathematician could not chalk 't out more plainly. And in this Discourse did [2] this most Superlative Theologue beat his brains for eight whole moneths, that at this hour he's as blind as a Beetle, to wit, all the sight of his eyes being run into the sharpness of his wit. But

[1] Quorsum haec tam putida tendunt ?   [2] θεολογώτατος ille.

for all that he nothing forthinketh his blindness, rather taking the same for too cheap a price of such a glory as he wan thereby.

And besides him I met with another, some eighty years of age, and such a Divine that you'd have sworn Scotus himself was reviv'd in him. He, being upon the point of unfolding the Mystery of the name Jesus, did with wonderful subtilty demonstrate that there lay hidden in those Letters what ever could be said of him ; for that it was only declin'd with three Cases, he said, it was a manifest token of the Divine Trinity ; and then, that the first ended in S, the second in M, the third in U, there was in it [1] an ineffable Mystery, to wit, those three Letters declaring to us that he was [2] the Beginning, Middle, and End of all. Nay, the Mystery was yet more abstruse ; for he so Mathematically split the word Jesus into two equal parts, that he left the middle letter by it self, and then told us that that letter in Hebrew was (ש) *Schin* or *Sin*, and that *Sin* in the Scotch tongue, as he remember'd, signifi'd as much as Sin ; from

[1] ἄρρητον.   [2] summum, medium et ultimum.

whence he gather'd that it was Jesus that took
away the sins of the world. At which new
Exposition the Auditory were so wonderfully
intent and struck with admiration, especially
the Theologues, that there wanted little but
that Niobe-like they had been turn'd to stones ;
whereas the like had almost happen'd to me, as
befell the Priapus in Horace. And not without
cause, for when were the Grecian Demosthenes
or Roman Cicero e're guilty of the like ? They
thought that Introduction faulty that was wide
of the Matter, as if it were not the way of
Carters and Swinheards, that have no more wit
than God sent 'em. But these learned men
think their Preamble, for so they call it, then
chiefly Rhetorical when it has least Coherence
with the rest of the Argument, that the admiring
Auditory may in the mean while whisper to
themselves, [1] 'What will he be at now ' ? In the
third place, they bring in instead of Narration
some Texts of Scripture, but handle 'em
cursorily, and as it were by the bye, when yet
it is the onely thing they should have insisted
on. And fourthly, as it were changing a Part

[1] Quo nunc se proripit ille ?

in the Play, they bolt out with some question in Divinity, and many times [1] relating neither to Earth nor Heaven, and this they look upon as a piece of Art. Here they erect their Theological Crests, and beat into the people's ears those Magnifical Titles of Illustrious Doctors, Subtile Doctors, most Subtile Doctors, Seraphick Doctors, Cherubin-Doctors, Holy Doctors, Unquestionable Doctors, and the like ; and then throw abroad among the ignorant people Syllogisms, Majors, Minors, Conclusions, Corollaries, Suppositions, and those so weak and foolish that they are below Pedantry. There remaines yet the fifth Act, in which one would think they should shew their Mastery. And here they bring in some foolish insipid Fable out of *Speculum Historiale* or *Gesta Romanorum*, and Expound it Allegorically, Tropologically, and Anagogically. And after this manner do they end their Chimæra, and such as Horace despair'd of compassing, when he writ ' Humano capiti,' &c.

But they have heard from some body, I know not whom, that the beginning of a Speech

---

[1] *οὔτε γῆς οὔτε οὐρανοῦ ἁπτομένην.*

should be Sober and Grave, and least given to noise. And therefore they begin theirs at that rate they can scarce hear themselves, as if it were no matter whether any one understood 'em. They have learnt some where that to move the affections a lowder voice is requisite. Whereupon they that otherwise would speak like a Mouse in a Cheese, start out of a suddain into a downright fury, even there too, where there's the least need of it. A man would swear they were past the power of Hellebor, so little do they consider where 'tis they run out. Again, because they have heard that as a Speech comes up to something, a man should press it more earnestly, they, how ever they begin, use a strange contention of voice in every part, though the Matter it self be never so flat, and end in that manner as if they'd run themselves out of breath. Lastly, they have learnt that among Rhetoricians there is some mention of Laughter, and therefore they study to prick in a jest here and there ; but, O Venus ! so void of wit and so little to the purpose, that it may be truly call'd [1] an Asses playing on the Harp. And sometimes

---

[1] Ὄνον πρὸς τὴν λύραν.

also they use somewhat of a sting, but so nevertheless that they rather tickle than wound ; nor do they ever more truly flatter than when they would seem [1] to use the greatest freedom of speech. Lastly, such is their whole action that a man would swear they had learnt it from our common Tumblers, though yet they come short of 'em in every respect. However, they are both so like, that no man will dispute but that either these learnt their Rhetorick from them, or they theirs from these. And yet they light on some that, when they hear 'em, conceive they hear very Demosthenes and Ciceroes : of which sort chiefly are our Merchants and Women, whose Ears onely they endeavour to please, because as to the first, if they stroake 'em handsomely, some part or other of their ill-gotten goods is wont to fall to their share. And the Women, though for many other things they favour this Order, this is not the least, that they commit to their breasts what ever discontents they have against their Husbands. And now, I conceive me, ye see how much this kind of people are beholding to me, that with their Petty Ceremonies,

[1] παῤῥησιάζεσθαι.

Ridiculous Trifles, and Noise, exercise a kind of Tyranny among mankind, believing themselves very Pauls and Anthonies.

But I willingly give over these Stage-players, that are such ingrateful dissemblers of the courtesies I have done 'em, and such impudent pretenders to Religion which they ha' n't. And now I have a mind to give some small touches of Princes and Courts, of whom I am had in reverence, above-board and, as it becomes Gentlemen, frankly. And truly, if they had the least proportion of sound judgment, what life were more unpleasant than theirs, or so much to be avoided ? For who ever did but truly weigh with himself how great a burthen lies upon his shoulders that would truly discharge the duty of a Prince, he would not think it worth his while to make his way to a Crown by Perjury and Parricide. He would consider that he that takes a Scepter in his hand should manage the Publick, not his Private Interest ; study nothing but the common good ; and not in the least go contrary to those Laws whereof himself is both the Author and Exactor : that he is to take an account of the good or evil administration of all his magistrates and subordinate Officers ; that, though he is but one, all men's Eyes are upon him, and in his power it is, either like a good Planet to give life and safety to mankind by his harmless influence, or like a fatal Comet to send mischief and destruction : that the vices of other men are not alike felt, nor so generally communicated ; and that a Prince stands in that place that his least deviation from the Rule of Honesty and Honour reaches farther than himself, and opens a gap to many men's ruine. Besides, that the fortune of Princes has many things attending it that are but too apt to train 'em out of the way, as Pleasure, Liberty, Flattery, Excess ; for which cause he should the more diligently endeavour and set a watch o're himself, lest perhaps he be led aside and fail in his duty. Lastly, to say nothing of Treasons, ill will and such other Mischiefs he's in jeopardy of, that that True King is over his head, who in a short time will cal him to account for every the least trespass, and that so much the more severely, by how much more mighty was the Empire committed to his charge. These and the like if a Prince should duly weigh, and weigh it he would if he were wise, he would neither be able to sleep nor take any hearty repast.

But now by my courtesie they leave all this care to the Gods, and are onely taken up with themselves, not admitting any one to their eare but such as know how to speak pleasant things, and not trouble 'em with business. They believe they have discharg'd all the duty of a Prince if they Hunt every day, keep a Stable of fine Horses, sell Dignities and Commanderies, and invent new wayes of draining the Citizens' Purses and bringing it into their own Exchequer ; but under such dainty new-found names, that though the thing be most injust in it self, it carries yet some face of equity ; adding to this some little sweetnings, that what ever happens, they may be secure of the common people. And now suppose some one, such as they sometimes are, a man ignorant of Laws, little less than an enemy to the publique good, and minding nothing but his own, given up to Pleasure, a hater of Learning, Liberty, and Justice, studying nothing less than the publique safety, but measuring every thing by his own will and profit ; and then put on

him a golden Chain, that declares the accord of
all Vertues linkt one to another; a Crown set
with Diamonds, that should put him in mind
how he ought to excell all others in Heroick
Vertues; besides a Scepter, the Emblem of
Justice and an untainted heart; and lastly, a
Purple Robe, a Badge of that Charity he owes the
Common-wealth. All which if a Prince should
compare 'em with his own life, he would I
believe be clearly asham'd of his bravery, and be
afraid lest some or other gibing Expounder turn
all this Tragical Furniture into a ridiculous
Laughing-stock.

And as to the Court-Lords, what should
I mention them? than most of whom though
there be nothing more indebted, more servile,
more witless, more contemptible, yet they would
seem as they were the most excellent of all others.
And yet in this only thing no men more modest,
in that they are contented to wear about 'em
Gold, Jewels, Purple, and those other marks
of Vertue and Wisdome, but for the study of
the things themselves, they remit it to others;
thinking it happiness enough for them that they
can call the King Master, have learnt the cringe

à la mode, know when and where to use those
Titles of Your Grace, My Lord, Your Magnifi-
cence; in a word that they are past all shame and
can flatter pleasantly.   For these are the Arts
that speak a man truly Noble and an exact
Courtier.   But if ye look into their manner of
life you'll find 'em meer Sots, [1] as debaucht as
Penelope's Wooers ; you know the other part
of the verse, which the Echo will better tell ye
than I can.   They sleep till noon, and have their
mercenary Levite come to their bed side, where
he chops over his Mattins before they are half
up.   Then to Break-fast, which is scarce done
but Dinner staies for 'em.   From thence they
go to Dice, Tables, Cards, or entertain themselves
with Jesters, Fools, Gambolls, and Horse-tricks.
In the mean time they have one or two Bevers,
and then Supper, and after that a Banquet,
and 'twere well, by Jupiter, there were no more
than one.   And in this manner do their Hours,
Dayes, Moneths, Years, Age slide away without
the least irksomeness.   Nay, I have sometimes
gone away many Inches fatter, to see 'em
[2] speak bigg words ; whiles each of the Ladies

---

[1] sponsos Penelopes, &c.   [2] μεγαλορρουντας.

believes her self so much nearer to the Gods, by how much the longer train she trails after her; whiles one Nobleman edges out another, that he may get the nearer to Jupiter himself; and every one of 'em pleases himself the more by how massier is the Chain he swaggs on his shoulders, as if he meant to shew his strength as well as his wealth.

Nor are Princes by themselves in their manner of life, since Popes, Cardinals, and Bishops have so diligently follow'd their steps, that they've almost got the start of 'em. For if any of 'em would consider what their Albe should put 'em in mind of, to wit a blameless life; what is meant by their forked Miters, whose each point is held in by the same knot, wee'll suppose it a perfect knowledge of the Old and New Testaments; what those Gloves on their Hands, but a sincere administration of the Sacraments, and free from all touch of worldly business; what their Crosier, but a careful looking after the Flock committed to their charge; what the Cross born before 'em, but victory over all earthly affections:—these, I say, and many of the like kind should any one

truly consider, would he not live a sad and
troublesome life? Whereas now they do well
enough while they feed themselves onely; and
for the care of their Flock, either put it over
to Christ or lay it all on their Suffragans, as
they call 'em, or some poor Vicars. Nor do they
so much as remember their name, or what the
word Bishop signifies; to wit, Labour, Care
and Trouble. But in racking to gather moneys
they truly act the part of Bishops, [1] and herein
acquit themselves to be no blind Seers.

In like manner Cardinals, if they thought
themselves the successours of the Apostles, they
would likewise imagine that the same things
the other did are requir'd of them, and that
they are not Lords, but Dispensers of Spiritual
things, of which they must shortly give an
exact account. But if they also would a little
Philosophize on their Habit, and think with
themselves what's the meaning of their Linen
Rochet; is it not a remarkable and singular
integrity of life? what that inner Purple;
is it not an earnest and fervent love of God?
or what that outward, whose loose Plaits and

[1] οὐδ' ἀλαοσκοπιή.

long Train fall round his Reverence's Mule, and are large enough to cover a Camel; is it not Charity, that spreads it self so wide to the succour of all men ? that is, to Instruct, Exhort, Comfort, Reprehend, Admonish, compose Wars, resist wicked Princes, and willingly expend, not onely their Wealth but their very Lives for the Flock of Christ : though yet what need at all of wealth to them that supply the room of the poor Apostles ?—These things, I say, did they but duely consider, they would not be so ambitious of that Dignity ; or, if they were, they would willingly leave it and live a laborious, careful life, such as was that of the antient Apostles.

And for Popes, that supply the place of Christ, if they should endeavour to imitate His Life, to wit His Poverty, Labour, Doctrine, Cross, and contempt of Life, or should they consider what the name Pope, that is Father, or Holiness, imports, who would live more disconsolate than themselves ? or who would purchase that Chair with all his substance ? or defend it so purchast, with Swords, Poisons, and all force imaginable ? so great a profit would the access of Wisdom deprive him of ;—Wisdom did I say ? nay, the least corn of that Salt which Christ speaks of : so much Wealth, so much Honour, so much Riches, so many Victories, so many Offices, so many Dispensations, so much Tribute, so many Pardons ; such Horses, such Mules, such Guards, and so much Pleasure would it lose them. You see how much I have comprehended in a little : instead of which it would bring in Watchings, Fastings, Tears, Prayers, Sermons, good Endeavours, Sighs, and a thousand the like troublesome Exercises. Nor is this least considerable : so many Scribes, so many Copying Clerks, so many Notaries, so many Advocates, so many Promooters, so many Secretaries, so many Muletters, so many Grooms, so many Bankers : in short, that vast multitude of men that overcharge the Roman See—I mistook, I meant honour—, might beg their bread.

A most inhumane and abominable thing, and more to be execrated, that those great Princes of the Church and true Lights of the World should be reduc'd to a Staff and a Wallet. Whereas now, if there be any thing that requires their pains, they leave that to Peter and Paul that have leisure enough ; but if there be any thing of Honour or Pleasure, they take that to themselves. By which means it is, yet by my courtesie, that scarce any kind of men live more voluptuously or with less trouble ; as believing that Christ will be well enough pleas'd, if in their Mystical and almost mimical Pontificalibus, Ceremonies, Titles of Holiness and the like, and Blessing and Cursing, they play the parts of Bishops. To work Miracles is old and antiquated, and not in fashion now ; to instruct the people, troublesome ; to interpret the Scripture, Pedantick ; to pray, a sign one has little else to do ; to shed tears, silly and womanish ; to be poor, base ; to be vanquisht, dishonourable, and little becoming him that scarce admits even Kings to kiss his Slipper ; and lastly, to dye, uncouth ; and to be stretcht on a Cross, infamous.

Theirs are only those Weapons and sweet Blessings which Paul mentions, and of these truly they are bountiful enough : as Interdictions, Hangings, Heavy Burthens, Reproofs, Anathemas, Executions in Effigie, and that terrible Thunder-bolt of Excommunication, with

the very sight of which they sink men's Souls
beneath the bottom of Hell: which yet these
most holy Fathers in Christ and his Vicars hurl
with more fierceness against none than against
such as, by the instigation of the Devil, attempt
to lessen or rob 'em of Peter's Patrimony. When,
though those words in the Gospel, 'We have
left all, and follow'd Thee,' were his, yet they call
his Patrimony Lands, Cities, Tribute, imposts,
Riches; for which, being enflam'd with the love
of Christ, they contend with Fire and Sword,
and not without losse of much Christian blood,
and believe they have then most Apostolically
defended the Church, the Spouse of Christ,
when the enemy, as they call 'em, are valiantly
routed.   As if the Church had any deadlier
enemies than wicked Prelates, who not onely
suffer Christ to run out of request for want of
preaching him, but hinder his spreading by their
multitudes of Laws, meerly contriv'd for their
own profit, corrupt him by their forc'd Exposi-
tions, and murder him by the evil example of
their pestilent life.

Nay, further, whereas the Church of Christ
was founded in blood, confirm'd by blood, and

augmented by blood, now, as if Christ, who after his wonted manner defends his people, were lost, they govern all by the Sword. And whereas War is so Savage a thing that it rather befits Beasts than Men, so outragious that the very Poets feign'd it came from the Furies, so pestilent that it corrupts all men's manners, so injust that it is best executed by the worst of men, so wicked that it has no agreement with Christ; and yet, omitting all the other, they make this their onely business. Here you'll see decrepit old fellows acting the parts of young men, neither troubled at their costs nor weari'd with their labours, nor discourag'd at any thing, so they may have the liberty of turning Laws, Religion, Peace and all things else quite topsie turvie. Nor are they destitute of their learned Flatterers that call that palpable Madness Zeal, Piety, and Valour, having found out a new way by which a man may kill his brother without the least breach of that Charity which, by the command of Christ, one Christian owes another. And here, in troth, I'm a little at a stand whether the Ecclesiastical German Electors gave 'em this example, or rather took

it from 'em; who, laying aside their Habit,
Benedictions and all the like Ceremonies, so act
the part of Commanders that they think it
a mean thing, and least beseeming a Bishop,
to shew the least courage to God-ward unless
it be in a battle.

And as to the common Heard of Priests,
they account it a crime to degenerate from
the Sanctity of their Prelates. Heidah! how
Souldier-like they bussle about the *jus divinum*
of Titles, and how quick-sighted they are to
pick the least thing out of the Writings of the
Antients, wherewith they may fright the common
people, and convince 'em, if possible, that more
than a Tenth is due! Yet in the mean-time
it least comes in their heads how many things
are every where extant concerning that duty
which they owe the people. Nor does their
shorn Crown in the least admonish 'em that
a Priest should be free from all worldly desires,
and think of nothing but heavenly things.
Whereas on the contrary, these jolly fellows
say they have sufficiently discharg'd their Office
if they but any-how mumble over a few odd
Prayers, which, so help me, Hercules! I wonder

if any God either hear or understand, since they do neither themselves; especially when they thunder 'em out in that manner they are wont. But this they have in common with those of the Heathens, that they are vigilant enough to the harvest of their profit, nor is there any of 'em that is not better read in those Laws than the Scripture. Whereas if there be any thing burthensome, they prudently lay that on other men's shoulders, and shift it from one to t'other, as men toss a Ball from hand to hand; following herein the example of Lay Princes, who commit the Government of their Kingdoms to their Grand Ministers, and they again to others, and leave all study of Piety to the common people. In like manner the common people put it over to those they call Ecclesiasticks, as if themselves were no part of the Church, or that their vow in Baptism had lost its obligation. Again, the Priests that call themselves Secular, as if they were initiated to the world, not to Christ, lay the burthen on the Regulars; the Regulars on the Monks; the Monks that have more liberty, on those that have less; and all of 'em on the Mendicants; the Mendicants on the

Carthusians, amongst whom, if any where, this Piety lies buried, but yet so close that scarce any one can perceive it. In like manner the Popes, the most diligent of all others in gathering in the Harvest of mony, refer all their Apostolical work to the Bishops ; the Bishops to the Parsons ; the Parsons to the Vicars ; the Vicars to their brother Mendicants ; and they again throw back the care of the Flock on those that take the Wooll.

But it is not my business to sift too narrowly the lives of Prelates and Priests, for fear I seem to have intended rather a Satyr than an Oration, and be thought to tax good Princes while I praise the bad. And therefore, what I slightly taught before, has been to no other end but that it might appear that there's no man can live pleasant unless he be initiated to my Rites, and have me propitious to him. For how can it be otherwise, when Fortune, the great Directress of all Humane Affairs, and my self are so all one that she was always an enemy to those wise men, and on the contrary so favourable to Fools and careless fellows, that all things hit luckly to 'em ?

You have heard of that Timotheus, the most
fortunate General of the Athenians, of whom
came that Proverb, [1]'His Net caught fish, though
he were asleep'; and that, [2]'The Owl flies';
whereas these other hit properly, Wise men [3]'born
in the fourth moneth'; and again, [4]'He rides
Sejanus's his horse'; and [5]'gold of Tolouse',
signifying thereby the extremity of ill fortune.
But I forbear [6]the further threading of Proverbs,
lest I seem to have pilfer'd my friend Erasmus's
Adagies. Fortune loves those that have least wit
and most confidence, and such as like that saying
of Caeṣar, [7]'The Dye is thrown'. But Wisdome
makes men bashful, which is the reason that
those Wise men have so little to do, unless it
be with Poverty, Hunger, and Chimny-corners;
that they live such neglected, unknown and
hated lives: whereas Fools abound in money,
have the chief Commands in the Common-
wealth, and in a word, flourish every way. For
if it be a happiness [8]to please Princes, and to be

---

[1] Ἡ εὔδοντος κύρτος αἱρεῖ.   [2] Γλαῦξ ἵπταται.
[3] ἐν τετράδι γεννηθέντες.   [4] Equum habet Sejanum.
[5] Aurum Tolosanum.   [6] παροιμιάζεσθαι.
[7] Jacta est alea.   [8] Principibus placuisse viris.

conversant among those Golden and Diamond
Gods, what is more unprofitable than Wisdom,
or what is it these kind of men have, may more
justly be censur'd? If Wealth is to be got,
how little good at it is that Merchant like to do,
if following the Precepts of Wisdom he should
boggle at Perjury; or being taken in a lie,
blush; or in the least regard the sad scruples
of those Wise-men touching Rapine and Usury.
Again, if a man sue for Honours or Church-
Preferments, an Ass or wild Oxe shall sooner
get 'em than a Wise man. If a man's in love with
a young Wench, none of the least Humors in
this Comedy, they are wholly addicted to Fools,
and are afraid of a Wise man, and flie him as
they would a Scorpion. Lastly, whoever intend
to live merry and frolique, shut their doors
against Wise men, and admit any thing sooner.
In brief, go whither ye will, among Prelates,
Princes, Judges, Magistrates, Friends, Enemies,
from highest to lowest, and you'll find all things
done by money; which, as a Wise man con-
temns it, so it takes a special care not to come near
him. What shall I say? There is no measure
or end of my praises, and yet 'tis fit my Oration

have an end. And therefore I'll ev'n break off; and yet, before I do it, 'twill not be amiss if I briefly shew ye that there has not been wanting even great Authours that have made me famous, both by their Writings and Actions, lest perhaps otherwise I may seem to have foolishly pleas'd my self only, or that the Lawyers charge me that I have prov'd nothing. After their example, therefore, will I alleadge my proofs, that is to say, [1]nothing to the point.

And first, every man allows this Proverb, ' That where a man wants matter, he may best frame some '. And to this purpose is that Verse which we teach Children, [2] ' 'Tis the greatest wisdome to know when and where to counterfeit the Fool '. And now judge your selves what an excellent thing this Folly is, whose very counterfeit and semblance only has got such praise from the Learned. But more candidly does that fat plump [3] ' Epicurean bacon-hogg ', Horace, for so he calls himself, bid us [4] ' mingle our purposes with Folly '; and whereas he adds the word *brevem*,

---

[1] Οὐδὲν πρὸς ἔπος.

[2] Stultitiam simulare loco prudentia summa est.

[3] Epicuri de grege porcus.   [4] Misce stultitiam consiliis.

short, perhaps to help out the Verse, he might as well have let it alone; and agen, [1]''tis a pleasant thing to play the fool in the right season'; and in another place, he had rather [2] 'be accounted a dottrel and sot, than to be wise and made mouths at'. And Telemachus in Homer, whom the Poet praises so much, is now and then called νήπιος, Fool: and by the same name, as if there were some good fortune in 't, are the Tragedians wont to call Boyes and Striplings. And what does that sacred book of Iliads contain, but a kind of counter-scuffle between foolish Kings and foolish People? Besides, how absolute is that praise that Cicero gives of it! [3] ' All things are full of fools'. For who does not know that every good, the more diffusive it is, by so much the better it is?

But perhaps their authority may be of small credit among Christians. Wee'l therefore, if you please, support our praises with some Testimonies of holy Writ also; in the first place, neverthelesse, having forespoke our Theologues

---

[1] Dulce est desipere in loco.
[2] Delirus inersque videri, . . . Quam sapere et ringi.
[3] Stultorum plena sunt omnia.

that they'll give us leave to do it without
offence. And in the next, forasmuch as we
attempt a matter of some difficulty, and it may
be perhaps a little too sawcy to call back agen
the Muses from Helicon to so great a journey,
especially in a matter they are wholly strangers
to ; it will be more sutable, perhaps, while I
play the Divine and make my way through such
prickly quiddities, that I entreat the Soul of
Scotus, a thing more bristlely than either Por-
cupine or Hedg-hog, to leave his Scorbone a while
and come into my brest, and then let him go
whither he pleases, [1] or to the dogs. I could wish
also that I might change my countenance, or
that I had on the square Cap and the Cassock,
for fear some or other should impeach me of
theft, as if I had privily rifled our Masters' Desks,
in that I have got so much Divinity. But it
ought not to seem so strange, if after so long
and intimate an acquaintance and converse with
'em, I have pickt up somewhat ; when as that
Fig-tree-god Priapus, hearing his owner read
certain Greek words, took so much notice of 'em,
that he got 'em by heart ; and that Cock in

[1] vel ἐς κόρακας.

Lucian, by having liv'd long amongst men, became at last a master of their Language.

But to the point [1] under a fortunate direction. Ecclesiastes saith in his first Chapter, [2]'The number of fools is infinite'; and when he calls it infinite, does he not seem to comprehend all men, unlesse it be some few, whom yet 'tis a question whether any man ever saw? But more ingenuously does Jeremiah in his tenth Chapter confess it, saying, [3]'Every man is made a fool through his own wisdome'; attributing wisedom to God alone, and leaving folly to all men else: and agen, [4]'Let not man glory in his wisdome'. And why, good Jeremiah, would'st thou not have a man glory in his wisedom? Because, he'll say, he has none at all. But to return to Ecclesiastes, who, when he cries out, 'Vanity of Vanities, all is vanity!' what other thoughts had he, do ye believe, than that, as I said before, the life of man is nothing else but an enterlude of Folly? In which [5] he has added one voice more to that justly receiv'd praise of Cicero's, which

---

[1] bonis avibus.   [2] Stultorum infinitus numerus.
[3] Stultus omnis, &c.   [4] Nec glorietur homo, &c.
[5] Album addidit calculum.

I quoted before, viz. ' All things are full of
fools'. Agen, that wise Preacher that said, ' A
fool changes as the Moon, but a wise man is
permanent as the Sun', what else did he hint
at in it, but that all mankind are fools, and
the name of Wise onely proper to God ? For
by the Moon Interpreters understand humane
Nature, and by the Sun, God, the only Fountain of light ; with which agrees that which
Christ himself in the Gospel denies, that any
one is to be call'd good but one, and that is
God. And then if he is a fool that is not wise,
and every good man according to the Stoicks
is a wise man, it is no wonder if all mankind
be concluded under Folly. Again Solomon,
Chap. 15, ' Foolishnesse' saith he, ' is joy to
the Fool', thereby plainly confessing that
without folly there is no pleasure in life. To
which is pertinent that other, [1] ' He that
encreaseth knowledge, encreaseth grief ; and in
much understanding there is much indignation'.
And does he not plainly confess as much,
Chap. 7, ' The heart of the wise is where sadness
is, but the heart of fools follows mirth ' ? by

[1] Quis apponit scientiam, &c.

which you see, he thought it not enough to have
learnt wisedome, without he had added the
knowledge of me also. And if ye will not
believe me, take his own words, Chap. 1,[1] 'I gave
my heart to know wisdome and knowledge,
madnesse and folly'. Where, by the way, 'tis
worth your remark, that he intended me somewhat extraordinary, that he nam'd me last.
A Preacher writ it, and this you know is the
order among Church-men, that he that is first
in Dignity comes last in place, as mindful no
doubt, what ever they do in other things,
herein at least to observe the Evangelical
precept.

Besides, that Folly is more excellent than
Wisdom, the Son of Sirach, who ever he were,
clearly witnesseth, Chap. 44, whose words, so
help me Hercules! I shall not once utter
before you meet [2] my Induction with a sutable
answer, according to the manner of those in
Plato that dispute with Socrates. What things
are more proper to be laid up with care, such as
are rare and precious, or such as are common
and of no account? Why do you give me no

[1] Dedi cor meum, &c.   [2] εἰσαγωγὴν meam.

answer? Well, though ye should dissemble, the Greek Proverb will answer for ye, [1] 'Fowl Water is thrown out of doors'; which, if any man shall be so ungratious as to contemn, let him know 'tis Aristotle's, the god of our Masters'. Is there any of ye so very a Fool as to leave Jewels and Gold in the street? In troth, I think not; in the most secret part of your Houses; nor is that enough, if there be any Drawer in your Iron Chests more private than other, there ye lay 'em; but dirt ye throw out of doors. And therefore, if ye so carefully lay up such things as you value, and throw away what's vile and of no worth, is it not plain that Wisdom, which he forbids a man to hide, is of less account than Folly, which he commands him to cover? Take his own words, 'Better is the man that hideth his Folly than he that hideth his Wisdom'. Or what is that, when he attributes an upright mind without Craft or Malice to a Fool, when a wise man the while thinks no man like himself? For so I understand that in his Tenth Chap., [2] 'A Fool walking by the way, being a fool himself,

[1] ἐπὶ θύραις ὑδρίαν.   [2] In via stultus, &c,

supposes all men to be fools like him '. And is it
not a signe of great integrity to esteem every man
as good as himself, and when there is no one
that leans not too much to 'ther way, to be so
frank yet as to divide his praises with another ?
Nor was this great King asham'd of the Name,
when he says of himself that he is more foolish
than any man. Nor did Paul, that great Doctor
of the Gentiles, writing to the Corinthians,
unwillingly acknowledg it ; ' I speak ' saith he,
' like a fool. I am more.' As if it could be any
dishonour to excel in Folly.

But here I meet with a great noise of some that
endeavour [1] to peck out the Crows' eyes ; that
is, to blind the Doctors of our times, and smoak
out their eyes with new Annotations ; among
whom my friend Erasmus, whom for honour's
sake I often mention, deserves, [2] if not the first
place, yet certainly the second. O most foolish
instance, they cry, and well becoming Folly her
self ! The Apostle's meaning was wide enough
from what thou dream'st ; for he spake it not
in this sense, that he would have them believe
him a greater fool than the rest : but when he

[1] Cornicum oculos configere.   [2] si non Alpha, certe Beta.

had said, ' They are Ministers of Christ, the
same am I ', and by way of boasting herein, had
equal'd himself with to 'thers, he added this by
way of correction or checking himself, ' I am
more ' ; as meaning that he was not onely equal
to the rest of the Apostles in the work of the
Gospel, but somewhat superiour. And therefore, while he would have this receiv'd as a
Truth, lest nevertheless it might not relish their
eares as being spoken with too much Arrogance,
he foreshorten'd his Argument with the Vizard
of Folly, ' I speak like a fool ' ; because he knew
it was the Prerogative of fools to speak what they
list, and that too without offence. Whatever
he thought when he writ this, I leave it to
them to discuss ; for my own part, I follow those
fat, fleshie, and vulgarly approv'd Doctours,
with whom [1] by Jupiter ! a great part of the
learned had rather err than follow them that
understand the Tongues, though they are never
so much in the right. Not any of 'em make
greater account of [2] those smatterers at Greek
than if they were Dawes. Especially when a no
small Professor, whose name I wittingly conceal,

---

[1] νὴ τὸν Δία.   [2] Graeculos istos quam graculos.

lest those Choughs should chatter at me that
Greek Proverb I have so often mentioned, [1] 'an
Asse at a Harp', discoursing Magisterially and
Theologically on this Text, ' I speak as a fool,
I am more', drew a new Thesis ; and, which
without the height of Logick he could never have
done, made this new Subdivision—For I'll give
ye his own words, not onely in form but
matter also—, 'I speak like a fool' : that is, if
you look upon me as a fool for comparing my
self with those false Apostles, I shall seem yet
a greater fool by esteeming my self before 'em ;
though the same person a little after, as forgetting himself, runs off to another matter.

But why do I thus staggeringly defend my
self with one single instance ? As if it were
not the common priviledg of Divines to stretch
Heaven, that is Holy Writ, like a Cheverel ;
and when there are many things in St. Paul
that thwart themselves, which yet in their
proper place do well enough, if there be any
credit to be given [2] to St. Jerom, that was
Master of five Tongues. Such was that of his at
Athens, when having casually espi'd the inscrip-

---

[1] Ὄνος λύρας.   [2] Illi πενταγλώττῳ Hieronymo.

tion of that Altar, he wrested it into an Argument to prove the Christian Faith, and leaving out all the other words because they made against him, took notice onely of the two last, viz. [1] 'To the unknown God'; and those too, not without some alteration, for the whole Inscription was thus: 'To the Gods of Asia, Europe, and Africa; To the unknown and strange Gods'. And according to his example do [2] the Sons of the Prophets, who, forcing out here and there four or five Expressions and if need be corrupting the sense, wrest it to their own purpose; though what goes before and follows after, make nothing to the matter in hand, nay, be quite against it. Which yet they do with so happy an impudence, that oftentimes the Civilians envie them that faculty.

For what is it in a manner they may not hope for success in, when this great Doctour (I had almost bolted out his name, but that I once agen stand in fear of the Greek Proverb) has made a construction on an expression of Luke, so agreeable to the mind of Christ as are Fire and Water to one another. For when the last point of danger was at hand, at which time

---

[1] Ignoto Deo.   [2] οἱ τῶν θεολόγων παῖδες.

retainers and dependants are wont in a more
special manner to attend their Protectours, to
examine what strength they have, and prepare
[1] for the encounter ; Christ, intending to take
out of his Disciples' minds all trust and confidence in such like defence, demands of them
whether they wanted any thing, when he sent
them forth so unprovided for a journey, that
they had neither shoes to defend their feet from
the injuries of stones and briers, nor the provision of a scrip to preserve 'em from hunger.
And when they had denied that they wanted any
thing, he adds, ' But now, he that hath a bagg,
let him take it, and likewise a scrip ; and he
that hath none, let him sell his coat and buy
a sword '.   And now when the summe of
all that Christ taught [2] prest onely Meekness,
Suffering and Contempt of life, who does not
clearly perceive what he means in this place ?
to wit, that he might the more disarm his
Ministers, that neglecting not onely Shoos and
Scrip but throwing away their very Coat, they
might, being in a manner naked, the more readily
and with less hindrance take in hand the work of

[1] συμμαχεῖν.   [2] inculcet.

the Gospel, and provide themselves of nothing but a sword : not such as Thieves and Murtherers go up and down with, but the Sword of the Spirit, that pierceth the most inward parts, and so cuts off as it were at one blow, all earthly affections, that they mind nothing but their duty to God. But see, I pray, whither this famous Theologue wrests it. By the Sword he interprets defence against persecution ; and by the Bagg sufficient provision to carry it on. As if Christ having alter'd his mind, in that he sent out his Disciples not so royally attended as he should have done, repented himself of his former instructions : or as forgetting that he had said, ' Blessed are ye when ye are evil spoken of, despised, and persecuted, &c.', and forbad 'em to resist evil ; for that the meek in Spirit, not the proud, are blessed : or, lest remembring, I say, that he had compar'd them to Sparrows and Lillies, thereby minding them what small care they should take for the things of this life, was so far now from having them go forth without a Sword, that he commanded 'em to get one, though with the sale of their Coat, and had rather they should go naked than want a brawl-

ing-iron by their sides. And to this, as under
the word ' Sword ', he conceives to be comprehended whatever appertains to the repelling
of injuries ; so under that of ' Scrip ' he takes
in whatever is necessary to the support of life.
And so does this deep Interpreter of the divine
meaning bring forth the Apostles to preach the
Doctrine of a crucified Christ, but furnisht at
all points with Launces, Slings, Quarter-staffs,
and Bombards ; lading 'em also with bag and
baggage, lest perhaps it might not be lawful
for 'em to leave their Inn unlesse they were
empty and fasting. Nor does he take the least
notice of this, that he that so will'd the Sword
to be bought, reprehends it a little after and
commands it to be sheath'd ; and that it was
never heard that the Apostles ever us'd or
swords or bucklers against the Gentiles, though
'tis likely they had don 't, if Christ had ever
intended, as this Doctor interprets.

There is another, too, whose name out of
respect I pass by, a man of no small repute, who
from those Tents which Habbakkuk mentions,
[1]'The Tents of the land of Midian shall tremble',

---

[1] Turbabuntur pelles, &c.

drew this Exposition, that it was prophesied of the skin of Saint Bartholomew, who was flay'd alive. And why, forsooth, but because those Tents were cover'd with skins? I was lately my self at a Theological dispute, for I am often there, where when one was demanding, What authority there was in holy Writ that commands Hereticks to be convinc'd by Fire rather than reclaim'd by Argument, a crabbed old fellow, and one whose supercilious gravity spake him at least a Doctor, answered in a great fume that Saint Paul had decreed it, who said, [1] 'Reject him that is a Heretick, after once or twice admonition'. And when he had sundry times, one after another, thundred out the same thing, and most men wondred what ailed the man, at last he explain'd it thus, making two words of one: [2] 'A Heretick must be put to death'. Some laught, and yet there wanted not others to whom this Exposition seem'd plainly Theological; which, when some, though those very few, oppos'd, they cut off the dispute, [3] as we

---

[1] Haereticum hominem post unam et alteram correptionem devita.　　[2] Devita, hoc est de vita, tollendum haereticum.
[3] Tenedia bipenni.

say, with a Hatchet, and the credit of so
uncontroulable an Author. 'Pray conceive me',
said he ; ' it is written, "Thou shalt not suffer
a witch to live". But every Heretick bewitches
the people ; therefore, &c.' And now, as many
as were present admir'd the man's wit, and
consequently submitted to his decision of the
Question. Nor came it into any of their heads
that that Law concern'd onely Fortune-tellers,
Enchanters, and Magicians, whom the Hebrews
call in their Tongue [1] 'Mecaschephim ', Witches
or Sorcerers : for otherwise, perhaps, by the
same reason it might as well have extended to
fornication and drunkenness.

But I foolishly run on in these matters, though
yet there are so many of 'em that neither
Chrysippus' nor Didymus's Volums are large
enough to contain 'em. I would onely desire ye
to consider this, that if so great Doctors may
be allow'd this liberty, you may the more
reasonably pardon even me also, [2] a raw,
effeminate Divine, if I quote not every thing
so exactly as I should. And so at last I return
to Paul. [3] ' Ye willingly ' saith he, ' suffer my

[1] מכשפים.   [2] συκίνη θεολόγῳ.   [3] Libenter, &c.

foolishness '; and again, ' Take me as a fool ' ;
and further, ' I speak it not after the Lord, but
as it were foolishly '; and in another place,
' We are fools for Christ's sake '. You have heard
from how great an Author how great praises
of Folly ; and to what other end, but that
without doubt he look'd upon 't as that one
thing both necessary and profitable. ' If any one
amongst ye ' saith he, ' seem to be wise, let him
be a fool, that he may be wise '. And in Luke,
Jesus cal'd those two Disciples, with whom he
joyn'd himself upon the way, ' fools '. Nor can
I give ye any reason why it should seem so strange,
when Saint Paul imputes a kind of folly even to
God himself. [1] ' The foolishness of God ' saith
he, 'is wiser than men.' Though yet I must confess that Origen upon the place denies that this
foolishness may be resembled to the uncertain
judgment of men ; of which kind is, that [2] ' the
preaching of the cross is to them that perish
foolishness '.

But why am I so careful to no purpose, that
I thus run on to prove my matter by so many
testimonies ? when in those mystical Psalms,

[1] Quod stultum est Dei, &c.   [2] Verbum crucis, &c.

Christ speaking to the Father sayes openly,
[1] ' Thou knownest my foolishnesse '. Nor is it
without ground that fools are so acceptable to
God. The reason perhaps may be this, that as
Princes carry a suspicious eye upon those that
are over-wise, and consequently hate 'em—as
Caesar did Brutus and Cassius, when he fear'd
not in the least drunken Antony; so Nero,
Seneca; and Dionysius, Plato—, and on the
contrary are delighted in those blunter and
unlabour'd wits; in like manner Christ ever
abhors and condemns [2] those wise men, and such
as put confidence in their own wisdome. And
this Paul makes clearly out when he said, [3] ' God
hath chosen the foolish things of this world ';
and when he saith, ' It pleased God by foolishness to save the world ', as well knowing it had
been impossible to have reform'd it by wisdome.
Which also he sufficiently declares himself,
crying out by the mouth of his Prophet, ' I will
destroy the wisedom of the wise, and cast away
the understanding of the prudent '.

And agen, when Christ gives Him thanks that

---

[1] Tu scis insipientiam meam.   [2] σοφοὺς istos,

[3] Quae stulta sunt mundi, &c.

he had conceal'd the Mystery of Salvation from
the wise, but revealed it to babes and sucklings,
that is to say, Fools. For the Greek word for
Babes is [1] Fools, which he opposeth to the word
[2] Wise men. To this appertains that throughout
the Gospel you find him ever accusing the
Scribes and Pharisees and Doctors of the Law,
but diligently defending the ignorant multitude
(for what other is that ' Woe to ye Scribes and
Pharises ', than woe to ye, ye wise men ?),
but seems chiefly delighted in little Children,
Women, and Fishers. Besides, among brute
Beasts he is best pleas'd with those that have
least in 'em of the Foxes subtilty. And therefore he chose rather to ride upon an Asse, when,
if he had pleas'd, he might have bestrid the
Lion without danger. And the Holy Ghost
came down in the shape of a Dove, not of an
Eagle or Kite. Add to this that in Scripture
there is frequent mention of Harts, Hinds and
Lambs ; and such as are destin'd to eternal life
are called sheep, than which creature there is
not any thing more foolish ; if we may believe
that Proverb of Aristotle [3] ' sheepish manners ',

[1] $\nu\eta\pi\iota\text{οις}$.   [2] $\sigma\text{οφ}\text{οῖς}$.   [3] $\pi\rho\text{οβάτειον}\ \hat{\eta}\theta\text{ος}$.

which he tells us is taken from the foolishness of that creature, and is us'd to be apply'd to dull-headed people and lack-wits. And yet Christ professes to be the Shepheard of this Flock, and is himself delighted with the name of a Lamb ; according to Saint John, ' Behold the Lamb of God ! ' Of which also there is much mention in the Revelation. And what does all this drive at, but that all mankind are fools— nay, even the very best ?

And Christ himself, that he might the better relieve this Folly, being the wisdome of the Father, yet in some manner became a fool, when taking upon him the nature of man, he was found in shape as a man ; as in like manner he was made Sin, that he might heal sinners. Nor did he work this Cure any other way than by the foolishness of the Cross, and a company of fat Apostles, not much better, to whom also he carefully recommended folly, but gave 'em a caution against wisdome, and drew 'em together by the Example of little Children, Lillies, Mustard-seed and Sparrows, things senseless and inconsiderable, living only by the dictates of Nature and without either craft or care. Besides, when he forbad 'em to be troubled about what they should say before Governors, and straightly charg'd 'em not to enquire after times and seasons, to wit, that they might not trust to their own wisedom but wholly depend on him. And to the same purpose is it that that great Architect of the World, God, gave man an Injunction against his eating of the Tree of Knowledge, as if knowledge were the bane of happinesse ; according to which also, St. Paul dis-allows it as puffing up and destructive; whence also St. Bernard seems in my opinion to follow, when he interprets that mountain whereon Lucifer had fixt his habitation, to be the mountain of knowledge.

Nor perhaps ought I to omit this other argument, that folly is so gracious above, that her errors are only pardoned, those of wise men never. Whence it is that they that ask forgiveness, though they offend never so wittingly, cloak it yet with the excuse of folly. So Aaron, in Numbers, if I mistake not the book, when he sues unto Moses concerning his Sister's leprosie, [1] ' I beseech thee, my Lord, not to lay this sin

[1] Obsecro, Domine mi, &c.

upon us, which we have foolishly committed '. So Saul makes his excuse to David, ' For behold ', saith he, 'I did it foolishly'. And again, David himself thus sweetens God, ' And therefore I beseech thee, O Lord, to take away the trespass of thy Servant, for I have done foolishly '; as if he knew there was no pardon to be obtain'd unlesse he had colour'd his offence with folly and ignorance. And stronger is that of Christ upon the Cross when he pray'd for his enemies, ' Father forgive them '; nor does he cover their crime with any other excuse than that of un-wittingnesse—because, saith he, ' they know not what they do '. In like manner Paul, writing to Timothy, ' But therefore I obtain'd mercy, for that I did it ignorantly through unbelief '. And what is the meaning of ' I did it ignorantly ' but that I did it out of folly, not malice ? And what of, ' Therefore I receiv'd mercy ', but that I had not obtain'd it, had I not been made more allowable through the covert of folly ? For us also makes that mystical Psalmist, though I remembred it not in its right place, ' Remember not the sins of my youth nor my ignorances '. You see what two things he pretends, to wit,

Youth, whose companion I ever am, and Ignorances, and that in the plural number, a number of multitude, whereby we are to understand that there was no small company of 'em.

But not to run too far in that which is infinite. To speak briefly, all Christian Religion seems to have a kind of allyance with folly, and in no respect to have any accord with wisedom. Of which if ye expect proofs, consider first that boyes, old men, women and fools are more delighted with religious and sacred things than others, and to that purpose are ever next the Altars ; and this they do by meer impulse of Nature. And in the next place, you see that those first founders of it were plain, simple persons, and most bitter enemies of Learning. Lastly there are no sort of fools seem more out of the way than are these whom the zeal of Christian Religion has once swallow'd up ; so that they waste their estates, neglect injuries, suffer themselves to be cheated, put no difference between friends and enemies, abhor pleasure, are cram'd with poverty, watchings, tears, labours, reproaches, loathe life, and wish death above all things ; in short, they seem senseless to common understanding, as if their

minds liv'd elsewhere and not in their own
bodies ; which, what else is it than to be mad ?
For which reason you must not think it so strange
if the Apostles seem'd to be drunk with new wine,
and if Paul appear'd to Festus to be mad.

But now, having once gotten on [1] the Lion's
skin, go to, and I'll shew ye that this happinesse
of Christians, which they pursue with so much
toil, is nothing else but a kind of madnesse and
folly ; far be it that my words should give any
offence, rather consider my matter. And first,
the Christians and Platonicks do as good as agree
in this, that the Soul is plung'd and fetter'd
in the prison of the body, by the grossnesse of
which it is so ty'd up and hinder'd, that it cannot
take a view of or enjoy things as they truly are ;
and for that cause their master defines Philosophy
to be a contemplation of death, because it takes
off the mind from visible and corporeal objects,
than which death does no more. And therefore,
as long as the Soul useth the Organs of the
Body in that right manner it ought, so long it
is said to be in good state and condition ; but
when, having broke its fetters, it endeavours to

[1] τὴν λεοντῆν.

get loose, and assayes, as it were, a flight out of
that prison that holds it in, they call it madness;
and if this happen through any distemper, or
indisposition of the organs, then, by the common
consent of every man, 'tis down-right madnesse.
And yet we see such kind of men foretell things
to come, understand Tongues and Letters they
never learnt before, and seem, as it were, big with
a kind of Divinity.   Nor is it to be doubted but
that it proceeds from hence, that the mind, being
somewhat at liberty from the infection of the
body, begins to put forth it self in its native
vigour.   And I conceive 'tis from the same cause
that the like often happens to sick men a little
before their death, that they discourse in strain
above mortality, as if they were inspir'd.   Agen,
if this happens upon the score of Religion,
though perhaps it may not be the same kind of
madness, yet 'tis so near it that a great many
men would judge it no better, especially when a
few inconsiderable people shall differ from the
rest of the world in the whole course of their life.
And therefore it fares with them, as, according
to the Fiction of Plato, happens to those that
being coopt up in a cave stand gaping with

admiration at the shadows of things ; and that fugitive who, having broke from 'em and returning to 'em agen, told 'em he had seen things truly as they were, and that they were the most mistaken in believing there was nothing but pitiful shadows. For as this wise man pitty'd and bewail'd their palpable madness that were possest with so grosse an error, so they in return laught at him as a doating fool, and cast him out of their company. In like manner the common sort of men chiefly admire those things that are most corporeal, and almost believe there is nothing beyond 'em. Whereas on the contrary, these devout persons, by how much the nearer any thing concerns the body, by so much the more they neglect it, and are wholly hurry'd away with the contemplation of things invisible. For the one give the first place to riches, the next to their corporal pleasures, leaving the last place to their soul ; which yet most of 'em do scarce believe, because they can't see it with their eyes. On the contrary, the others first rely wholly on God, the most unchangeable of all things ; and next him, yet on this that comes nearest him, they bestow the second on their

soul; and lastly, for their body, they neglect
that care, and contemn and fly monies as super-
fluity that may be well spar'd; or if they are
forc't to meddle with any of these things, they
do it carelesly and much against their wills,
having as if they had it not, and possessing as
if they possessed it not.

There are also in each several things several
degrees wherein they disagree among themselves.
And first as to the senses, though all of 'em have
more or lesse affinity with the body, yet of these
some are more gross and blockish, as tasting,
hearing, seeing, smelling, touching; some more
remov'd from the body, as memory, intellect,
and the will. And therefore to which of these
the mind applies its self, in that lyes its force.
But holy men, because the whole bent of their
minds is taken up with those things that are
most repugnant to these grosser senses, they seem
brutish and stupid in the common use of them.
Whereas on the contrary, the ordinary sort of
people are best at these, and can do least at
to'ther; from whence it is, as we have heard,
that some of these holy men have by mistake
drunk oil for wine. Agen, in the affections of

the mind, some have a greater commerce with
the body than others, as lust, desire of meat and
sleep, anger, pride, envy ; with which holy men
are at irreconcilable enmity, and contrary, the
common people think there's no living without
'em. And lastly there are certain middle kind
of affections, and as it were natural to every man,
as the love of one's Country, Children, Parents,
Friends, and to which the common people
attribute no small matter ; whereas to'ther strive
to pluck 'em out of their mind : unlesse insomuch
as they arrive to that highest part of the soul,
that they love their Parents not as Parents—for
what did they get but the body ? though yet we
owe it to God, not them—but as good men or
women, and in whom shines the Image of
that highest wisdom, which alone they call the
chiefest good, and out of which, they say, there
is nothing to be belov'd or desir'd.

And by the same rule do they measure all
things else, so that they make lesse account of
whatever is visible, unlesse it be altogether
contemptible, than of those things which they
cannot see. But they say that in Sacraments and
other religious Duties there is both body and

Spirit. As in fasting they count it not enough for a man to abstain from eating, which the common people take for an absolute Fast, unlesse there be also a lessening of his deprav'd affections : as that he be lesse angry, less proud, than he was wont, that the Spirit, being less clog'd with its bodily weight, may be the more intent upon heavenly things. In like manner, in the Eucharist, though, say they, it is not to be esteem'd the less that 'tis administer'd with Ceremonies, yet of its self 'tis of little effect, if not hurtful, unless that which is spiritual be added to it, to wit, that which is represented under those visible signes. Now the death of Christ is represented by it, which all men, vanquishing, abolishing and, as it were, burying their carnal affections, ought to express in their lives and conversations, that they may grow up to a new-ness of life, and be one with him, and the same one amongst another. This a holy man does, and in this is his only meditation. Whereas on the contrary, the common people think there's no more in that Sacrifice than to be present at the Altar, and crow'd next it, to have a noise of words and look upon the Ceremonies. Nor

in this alone, which we onely propos'd by way
of example, but in all his life, and without
hypocrisie, does a holy man fly those things that
have any alliance with the body, and is wholly
ravisht with things Eternal, Invisible, and
Spiritual. For which cause there's so great
contrariety of opinion between 'em, and that
too in every thing, that each party thinks the
other out of their wits ; though that character,
in my judgment, better agrees with those holy
men than the common people : which yet will
be more clear if, as I promis'd, I briefly shew ye
that that great reward they so much fancy is
nothing else but a kind of madness.

And therefore suppose that Plato dreamt of
somewhat like it when he call'd the madness of
Lovers the most happy condition of all others.
For he that's violently in Love lives not in his
own body, but in the thing he loves ; and by how
much the farther he runs from himself into
another, by so much the greater is his pleasure.
And then, when the mind strives to rove from its
body, and does not rightly use its own organs,
without doubt you may say 'tis downright madnesse and not be mistaken, or otherwise what's

the meaning of those common ·sayings, [1] ' He does not dwell at home ', ' Come to your self ', ' He's his own man again ' ? Besides, the more perfect and true his love is, the more pleasant is his madness. And therefore, what is that life hereafter, after which these holy minds so pantingly breathe, like to be? To wit, the Spirit shall swallow up the Body, as conqueror and more durable ; and this it shall do with the greater ease because heretofore, in its life-time, it had cleans'd and thinn'd it into such another nothing as its self. And then the Spirit agen shall be wonderfully swallow'd up by that highest mind, as being more powerful than infinite parts ; so that the whole man is to be out of himself, nor to be otherwise happy in any respect, but that being stript of himself, he shall participate of somewhat ineffable from that chiefest good that draws all things into its self. And this happiness though 'tis only then perfected when souls being joyn'd to their former bodies shall be made immortal, yet forasmuch as the life of holy men is nothing but a continu'd meditation and, as it were, shadow of that life, it so happens that

---

[1] Non est apud se : Ad te redi : Sibi redditus est.

at length they have some taste or relish of it ; which, though it be but as the smallest drop in comparison of that fountain of eternal happiness, yet it far surpasses all worldly delight, though all the pleasures of all mankind were all joyn'd together. So much better are things spiritual than things corporal, and things invisible than things visible ; which doubtless is that which the Prophet promiseth : 'The eye hath not seen, nor the ear heard, nor has it entred into the heart of man to consider what God has provided for them that love Him'. And this is that Mary's better part, which is not taken away by change of life, but perfected.

And therefore they that are sensible of it, and few there are to whom this happens, suffer a kind of somewhat little differing from madness ; for they utter many things that do not hang together, and that too not after the manner of men, but make a kind of sound which they neither heed themselves, nor is it understood by others, and change the whole figure of their countenance, one while jocund, another while dejected, now weeping, then laughing, and agen sighing. And when they come to themselves, tell ye they know not where they have been, whether in the body or out of the body, or sleeping ; nor do they remember what they have heard, seen, spoken or done, and only know this, as it were in a mist or dream, that they were the most happy while they were so out of their wits. And therefore they are sorry they are come to themselves agen, and desire nothing more than this kind of madnesse, to be perpetually mad. And this is a small taste of that future happiness.

But I forget my self and [1] run beyond my bounds. Though yet, if I shall seem to have spoken any thing more boldly or impertinently than I ought, be pleas'd to consider that not only Folly but a Woman said it ; remembring in the mean time that Greek Proverb, [2] ' Sometimes a fool may speak a word in season ', unlesse perhaps you'll say this concerns not Women. I see you expect an Epilogue, but give me leave to tell ye you are much mistaken if you think I remember any thing of what I have said, having foolishly bolted out such a hodg podg of words.

---

[1] ὑπὲρ τὰ ἐσκαμμένα πηδῶ.

[2] Πολλάκι τοι καὶ μωρὸς ἀνὴρ κατακαίριον εἶπεν.

'Tis an old Proverb, [1] ' I hate one that remembers what's done over the Cup '. This is a new one of my own making: [2] I hate a man that remembers what he hears. Wherefore farewell, clap your hands, live, and drink lustick, my most excellent Disciples of Folly.

ΤΕΛΟΣ.　FINIS

[1] Μισῶ μνάμονα συμπόταν.　　[2] Μισῶ μνάμονα ἀκροατήν.

GREAT BOOKS IN PHILOSOPHY PAPERBACK SERIES

ETHICS

Aristotle—*The Nicomachean Ethics*	$8.95
Marcus Aurelius—*Meditations*	5.95
Jeremy Bentham—*The Principles of Morals and Legislation*	8.95
John Dewey—*The Moral Writings of John Dewey,*	
Updated and Revised Edition (edited by James Gouinlock)	10.95
Epictetus—*Enchiridion*	3.95
Immanuel Kant—*Fundamental Principles of the*	
Metaphysic of Morals	4.95
John Stuart Mill—*Utilitarianism*	4.95
George Edward Moore—*Principia Ethica*	8.95
Friedrich Nietzsche—*Beyond Good and Evil*	8.95
Bertrand Russell—*Bertrand Russell On Ethics, Sex, and Marriage*	
(edited by Al Seckel)	17.95
Benedict de Spinoza—*Ethics* and *The Improvement of the Understanding*	9.95

SOCIAL AND POLITICAL PHILOSOPHY

Aristotle—*The Politics*	7.95
Mikhail Bakunin—*The Basic Bakunin: Writings, 1869-1871*	
(translated and edited by Robert M. Cutler)	10.95
Edmund Burke—*Reflections on the Revolution in France*	7.95
John Dewey—*Freedom and Culture*	10.95
G. W. F. Hegel—*The Philosophy of History*	9.95
Thomas Hobbes—*The Leviathan*	7.95
Sidney Hook—*Paradoxes of Freedom*	9.95
Sidney Hook—*Reason, Social Myths, and Democracy*	11.95
John Locke—*Second Treatise on Civil Government*	4.95
Niccolo Machiavelli—*The Prince*	4.95
Karl Marx/Frederick Engels—*The Economic and Philosophic*	
Manuscripts of 1844 and *The Communist Manifesto*	6.95
John Stuart Mill—*Considerations on Representative Government*	6.95
John Stuart Mill—*On Liberty*	4.95
John Stuart Mill—*On Socialism*	7.95
John Stuart Mill—*The Subjection of Women*	4.95
Friedrich Nietzsche—*Thus Spake Zarathustra*	9.95

GREAT MINDS PAPERBACK SERIES

ECONOMICS

RELIGION

SCIENCE

HISTORY

SOCIOLOGY

(Prices subject to change without notice.)